THE
romantics

AMULET BOOKS
NEW YORK

THE
romantics

LEAH KONEN

Cataloging-in-Publication Data has been applied for and may be obtained from the Library of Congress.

ISBN: 978-1-4197-2193-9

Produced by Alloy Entertainment
1325 Avenue of the Americas
New York, NY 10019
www.alloyentertainment.com

Text copyright © 2016 Alloy Entertainment and Leah Konen
Jacket and interior illustrations copyright © 2016 Jordan Sondler
Book design by Alyssa Nassner

Printed and bound in the United States
10 9 8 7 6 5 4 3 2 1

Amulet Books are available at special discounts when purchased in quantity for premiums and promotions as well as fundraising or educational use. Special editions can also be created to specification. For details, contact specialsales@abramsbooks.com or the address below.

ABRAMS The Art of Books
115 West 18th Street, New York, NY 10011
abramsbooks.com

this book is dedicated to all the
romantics out there, you know who you are.

never stop believing.
(the rest of us depend on your optimism.)

Love's notes

NO, NOT LOVE NOTES. LOVE IN THE POSSESSIVE. I.E., notes from me.

I am Love. Your trusty narrator. Frequently referenced, usually misunderstood. Often imitated, never duplicated—that kind of thing.

That's why I'm here—ditching my cloak of mystery, talking to you straight—to tell you a love story. A real love story—one that actually involves me.

Before we get started, a few guidelines. A handbook, if you will—to the ways of Love.

Rule Number One:

I will never ask you to ingest poison, fall on your lover's sword, become a subhuman species, wage war, or generally cause yourself or others bodily harm. That's the stuff of books and stories, not the real deal.

Rule Number Two:

I may not give much warning. It is quite possible that I'm right around the corner and you have no idea. Sometimes even I don't know where I'll be next—I'm Love, not some all-knowing god.

Rule Number Three:

I cannot prevent you from going after the wrong person.

In fact, it is quite possible that you think you've found me when you haven't.

People manage to see me in the most ridiculous of places: in a stolen kiss with your best friend's boyfriend; in the soft words of the model-esque boy asking you to lose it on his basement couch. But this is True Love, you say—cue the music, soften the lighting, slap on a filter that makes you both look all dreamy and romantic!

Sorry to disappoint, but a lot of the time, that's not really me.

I refer you back to Rule Number One. Romeo and Juliet; Arthur, Lancelot, and Guinevere; Marc Antony and Cleopatra; Bella and Edward—history and literature are full of examples of people who have made bad decisions in the name of, well, me.

Look, humans make a lot of mistakes. I don't. Just trust me on this one.

I'm asking you to forget everything you know about *True Love*. The real kind doesn't make you selfish and short-sighted. Real love makes you better than you ever knew you could be.

So, how do you find me? Well, I'm actually the one who finds you. See below.

Rule Number Four:

I will be in your life at one point or another.

This is my promise to you, no matter if you have spar-kling green eyes or a face full of acne. No matter if you live in a Paris apartment overlooking the Seine or in rural

Indiana overlooking cows. When it's your turn, I'll be there. And I will help you, if you let me.

Rule Number Five:

I cannot control you—or the Harry Styles lookalike in your calculus class. When it comes to the important stuff, it's all on you.

That said, I've been known to give little, yet effective, nudges.

Rule Number Six:

Sometimes my timing is tricky.

Take Gael Brennan. He's a serious type, a kid with a plan. A Romeo, convinced he's found his Juliet. A high school senior in Chapel Hill, North Carolina, who has no earthly idea what's in store for him.

He's about to lose his faith in me. And what I hate to admit is that said faith-losing is at least partially my fault, if you can believe it. I know, I know, I said I don't make mistakes.

And I don't.

Well, I *didn't*.

But I'm going to do everything in my power to make this right.

Because there's a reason dear Gael needs me in his life. A big one. And let's just say it's *not* so he'll have someone to take to prom.

Of course, half the fun of my job is the challenge. Which brings me to—

Rule Number Seven:

I am allowed to get creative.

Before you protest, let me assure you that, as promised in Rule Number Five, human free will remains intact. I can't force people to do anything. I don't have a pouch full of arrows or a curio full of potions.

But that doesn't mean I don't have my ways . . .

throwback to the first
"i love you"

GAEL BIT AT HIS THUMB AS ALFRED HITCHCOCK'S *THE
Birds* ended in a shot of a landscape awash with feathers.

"Did you like it?" he asked Anika nervously. It was
entirely possible—likely, even—that she hadn't. Sure, they'd
already rented *Vertigo*, which she'd enjoyed. And she'd seen
Psycho on her own, but he'd always thought those were
easier to like. *The Birds* was just so much weirder. Of course,
Anika was pretty weird herself. But still.

"I did." Anika smiled, eating the last of the fun-size
Snickers bars she always pilfered when she came over and
squeezing closer to him on the couch. They were cuddled
up in the basement-slash-entertainment room, a comfy,
ugly space with wood paneling, faded posters, a discolored
rug that had somehow survived his dad's college dorm,
and a huge flat-screen TV. It was the only place that had
escaped his mom's meticulous decorating, holding none
of the charm of the rooms upstairs, and yet it was Gael's
favorite.

"I mean, you *may* have overhyped it a tad," Anika continued, pursing her lips. "But I'd expect nothing less." She
smiled, and Gael allowed himself to take her in: her dark

glossy hair pinned into thick braids around the crown of her head—looking like some kind of badass milkmaid; her wide-open eyes that grew two sizes bigger when she was being funny or making a point; her tiny, unassuming mouth. She was a perfect, beautiful girl, who was also offbeat enough to love this movie (almost) as much as he did.

The word *love* stuck in Gael's mind like a peanut butter sandwich to the roof of his mouth. So delicious and at the same time so uncomfortable. (Or so I'm told. From my position in the world, I don't exactly get to indulge in many PB&Js.)

It was September 18, one month to the day since they'd first kissed, something he would have made a big deal of, except Anika had gone on and on about how annoying it was when her best friend, Jenna, kept them posted on her relationship length just about every week.

He knew a month was fast to say it. And yet it felt so natural, so right.

Gael held her tighter as Anika nuzzled into his chest. Her body felt warm and soft against his. He and his family had spent countless hours watching movies on this ratty basement couch, but since his dad had moved out, he'd been watching them almost exclusively in his room. With Anika, it somehow felt okay to be down here again. There would always be the pang of what used to be, but now there was at least the promise of what *could* be, too.

Gael ran his hand over her braids as his eyes flitted to the clock on the Blu-ray player. It was past 9:30, and her curfew was ten on weekdays. Anika wasn't exactly the type to care much about curfew, but Gael was the type to want to show her parents how much he respected their rules.

Anika looked up at him mischievously. "Not exactly the most romantic movie." She smirked. "Though I suppose more romantic than the *Battlestar Galactica* marathon I imposed on you last week." She didn't drop her gaze. "I guess we'll just have to make up for it."

Anika ran her hands through his hair, her fingertips on his scalp making him shiver, and then pulled his lips to meet hers. Her kisses were fast and insistent, and in seconds, she was on his lap, straddling him on the couch.

Gael pulled away. "Hold on." Those pivotal three words burned in the back of his throat, where they'd been lodged for the past few days. Anika had already told him she had to study tomorrow night and wouldn't be able to come over, which meant that if he didn't say them soon, he'd have to wait another forty-eight hours.

And for a Romantic[1] like Gael, that was an unbearably long time.

Anika gave him a playful peck of a kiss. "Why? I promise I'm not a maniacal seagull in disguise." She kissed him again, then raised an eyebrow. "Or *am* I?"

---

1. Romantic: One who ruthlessly believes in love in its finest form and impresses those feelings onto his or her various relationships. May result in scaring off partners, falling for the wrong person, and desperately trying to turn life into a movie with glamorous Old Hollywood actors. May also result in some of the best, most inspiring, and deepest relationships around.

Gael laughed, then rested his hands on her hips and tried to ignore the urgency in his pants. Anika's face was flushed. She looked so startlingly beautiful, he knew that he couldn't *not* say it now.

"I wanted to tell you something," he said.

"That you're a maniacal seagull in disguise? I'm cool with it." She pulled him back toward her, clearly uninterested in talking.

He kissed her for a second and then pulled back again.

He felt like he was going to throw up, but in the best possible way. He felt a tingling in the tips of his fingers. He felt that he could do this right, even if his parents couldn't. He wondered how long it had been since he'd blinked. He knew it was now or never. (I, for one, prepared for what I knew would, inevitably, follow.)

"I just wanted to say that I love you."

I caught the flash of panic as it started across Anika's face, and I sent a strong gust of wind whipping through the tiny basement window. It tickled the edges of a Pokémon poster tacked precariously over the couch with years-old Scotch tape. In an instant, the poster fell on top of them.

Gael batted the poster away. "Are you okay?"

"I'm fine," Anika said quickly.

As I'd hoped, Anika took advantage of the interruption to compose her face. The panic was gone.

It was only then that Gael realized she hadn't said it back.

"No pressure to reciprocate or whatever. I know it's

only been a month . . . it's just that, well, I felt I had to say it."

Anika nodded.

"You're not super weirded out, are you?" Gael stared at the tattered poster on the couch beside them, Pikachu's frenzied, cheerful eyes gazing back. He forced himself to stop biting the inside of his cheek and picked at his thumbnail instead.

Anika hesitated an agonizing moment, but then she grabbed his chin, tilted his face back to hers.

"No." She kissed him long and deep. When she broke away, she was smiling again. "I'll see you this weekend, okay?"

Gael swore he saw hints of love in her eyes.

And I swore, too—because he never would have jumped in so quickly if it hadn't been for my mistake.

It wasn't go-time yet, but I knew that very soon I'd have to put my plan into action.

I couldn't wait.

the second-worst day of gael's life

EVEN THOUGH GAEL WAS LUGGING HIS HUGE TENOR sax, his steps felt light as he headed to the band room before school.

It was Tuesday, October 2—two weeks exactly since Gael told Anika he loved her (yes, he was counting). The leaves were beginning to turn and the temperature was starting to drop. Everything was as it should be: The world had not imploded due to his premature declaration.

Sure, Anika may not have said the words back yet, but she seemed to say it in other ways: when she texted him last thing before she went to sleep; when she reminded him of the AP calculus homework whenever he forgot to write it down; when she laced her fingers in his and gave his hand the tiniest squeeze . . .

(Difficult truth time: If people want to say "I love you" back, they will.)

Gael and Anika sometimes drove to school together, but she told him yesterday that all week she'd be getting there a half an hour early to practice her flute—she was going for first chair and the tryouts were on Friday. Today, however, he'd decided to surprise her and drive in early himself—and with flowers, no less. Red carnations. Anika loved red.

Gael crossed the mostly empty parking lot and headed through the courtyard and the back double doors, whose squeaks seemed extra loud in the morning quiet. The school felt weirdly calm this early. The hallways looked bigger in the absence of people; the lockers were all uniformly shut. Footprints in the dusty linoleum provided the only proof that hundreds of kids were normally packed in. Gael headed toward the main hallway and took a right toward the band room, flowers proudly in hand, but the bright, cluttered space held only a couple of guys on trumpet—no Anika. Gael put his sax away, adjusted the straps of his backpack, and looked at his watch. He was sure she said she'd be here by now, and he wondered if maybe she'd left something in the car.

Gael's steps were still light as he headed back through the double doors and traipsed across the concrete to the parking lot. It was brisk but sunny, a good day to be in love and do something nice for your girlfriend.

Anika's car was a few rows behind his—a beat-up butter-yellow Volvo that suited her perfectly—but she wasn't in it.

By the time he got back to the band room—where Anika still wasn't—more people were arriving and the halls were slowly and sleepily coming to life. He decided to try her locker.

Gael spotted her from down the hall. Her hair was

down: long and loose and wavy. Anika's ever-changing hair was one of the things that delighted Gael most about her.

As he picked up the pace, he saw someone standing behind Anika. Tall and muscly, with wide goofy eyes, shaggy hair, and a slightly slouched posture—Mason, Gael's best friend. Mason never got to school early. He was normally five to ten minutes late to first period and somehow got away with it because he was Mason, and everyone loved Mason.

Mason and Anika were looking at each other as Anika shut the door to her locker. She was so focused on him that she didn't even see Gael standing just a few feet away.

Gael had never been in a car wreck, but it was exactly how people described it—everything slowed down, all the details stood out—the time on the clock and the auto-tuned voice on the radio and the drawn-out screech before the crunch of aluminum and the smell of burning rubber and the flash of white.

That's how it was when his parents had told him they were separating.

And that's how it was now.

There was the slam of other lockers, clacking one after another; there were the piercing shrieks of a group of freshman girls; and there were Gael's eyes locked on Mason, as Mason leaned in, slowly, surely, and directly—like the swing of a pendulum going farther than it ever had before—and kissed Anika right on the lips.

(For what it's worth, I'd tried to soften the blow for dear

Gael. The fifteen-minute warning bell rang exactly twelve seconds earlier than it should have, and at about twice its usual volume. But it didn't make a difference. Anika and Mason couldn't take their eyes off each other.)

After countless agonizing seconds of kissing, Anika pulled back and said, "Stop it. I didn't talk to Gael yet."

Gael's body was rigid, and the words were out of his mouth almost without his control. "I'm right here."

Anika and Mason whipped around like misbehaving schoolchildren.

"Gael," Anika blurted out. "What are you doing here? You're never here this early."

"Neither is he." Gael spit the words at his friend. "I came to surprise you."

"Oh," she said, looking down at the flowers in Gael's hand. They were pointed at the floor, like even they had lost hope—Gael instantly felt ridiculous. He opened his backpack and shoved them in—he couldn't look at them anymore.

Mason shifted on his huge, long legs. "Listen, man . . ."

Anika snapped into action. "Gael, we should probably talk alone."

Mason hesitated, but then Anika narrowed her eyes at him and drew her lips together just like she did when she wanted Gael to stop talking about classic movies— apparently, the wordless language Gael and Anika shared belonged to Mason now.

Mason nodded and shuffled away. Part of Gael wanted

to chase after him, grab him, ask him what the hell he thought he was doing with her, but he couldn't tear his eyes away from Anika.

She took a deep breath, running her finger along the top slat of her locker. Then, fixing her eyes on him and holding his gaze, she gave him her "let's talk" face. It was one of the things Gael liked about her most, how serious she could be. Anika had gumption. Not a lot of high school girls had gumption.

Enough gumption to cheat on her boyfriend with his best friend, Gael wondered.

"What is going on?" he asked. "Are you, like, with Mason now? Are you joking?" To his embarrassment, he realized his voice was trembling.

Anika looked down to her scuffed-up red Mary Janes, the ones she'd found in Goodwill the day Gael scored a faded *Taxi Driver* shirt. "I'm sorry."

The first thing: a thump and a shaking all over, like an earthquake only Gael could feel.

The second thing: her eyes lifting to his in confirmation. Something so impossible it had occupied exactly zero percent of his mental space had actually happened, just like that.

The third thing: people on the periphery, staring. Flashes of humans who had nothing to do with him and Anika. Devon Johnson. Mark Kaplan. Amberleigh Shotwell, reigning first-chair flute in band. He suddenly wondered how many of these people had known this was happening—it wasn't as if Anika and Mason were exactly being discreet. Gael imagined them laughing at him over greasy cafeteria grilled cheese: stupid, starry-eyed Gael who didn't have a clue what his girlfriend and best friend were doing behind his back.

"You have to be kidding," he said, his voice wavering and the first tear spilling down his cheek. Gael couldn't believe she was doing this to him, especially after everything that had happened with his parents. It was like it was her personal mission to confirm his biggest fear: that love wasn't real. How could it be if two people who'd seemed happy for his entire life suddenly weren't?

"How long has this been going on?" he asked, desperately praying that what he'd just witnessed was a brief moment of weakness, a fluke.

Anika bit her lip. "I don't know," she said. "A week, I guess."

A week? Anika and Mason had been doing who knows what for an entire week?

Gael grabbed Anika's shoulder, hanging on as if for dear life, and wrestled to get control of himself. "Look, you're confused and freaked out by what I said. Maybe if we just talk about this. What do you say? We'll ditch first period." Gael had never ditched a period in his life. Anika had, though, when she had waited in line for Flaming Lips tickets.

Anika always got what she wanted. And now she no longer wanted him.

"No, Gael. I can't." She tried to shrug his hand off.

Instead of letting go, Gael grabbed her other arm, desperately looking into her face. "Please."

For a second, there was sympathy in her dark brown eyes, and Anika almost looked like she was going to change her mind, like she suddenly realized that trading what she and Gael had for whatever the hell was going on with Mason was the stupidest thing in the world. Then a commanding "Excuse me!" broke the moment, the onlookers quickly dispersed, and Mrs. Channing materialized, looking at Gael sternly through frameless glasses. "Is there a problem here?"

Gael let Anika go, surreptitiously wiped the moisture from his eyes, and shoved his wet hand in his jacket pocket, where he fingered a mini-pack of tissues that he hadn't remembered putting there. (You're welcome, Gael.)

"Anika?" Mrs. Channing asked.

Anika hesitated. She actually hesitated. "No," she said finally. Meekly. Un-Anika-ly.

Mrs. Channing turned to Gael. "Can I see you in my office, Gael?"

"I have to go to class," he said. His eyes flitted back to Anika.

"I'll write you a pass," Mrs. Channing said. "Come on."

So Gael followed her down the hall, biting the insides of his cheeks to stop himself from falling apart in front of everyone.

He glanced back at Anika, but instead of looking sympathetic, she was rushing to her first class without so much as a glance back.

Anika had always marched to the beat of her own drum. Only now, she was marching away from him.

a humiliating interlude in the guidance counselor's office

HANG IN THERE! READ A POSTER ON MRS. CHANNING'S wall, a stock image of an upside-down cat suspended on monkey bars. Next to it was a photo of a cat crumpled on the ground, white block letters over it: *haynging n ther is overated.*

"Is everything okay with you, Gael?"

Gael pressed his feet firmly into the dingy tiles of the tiny office and crumpled the tissue in his hand. His breathing was shaky. That morning, things had been so good—or as good as they could be, under the circumstances. He was a senior. He had a decent shot of getting accepted to UNC. He had Anika. He had Mason.

Sure, he was hoping against hope that his parents would get their act together and his dad would move back in, but his relationship with Anika had distracted him from all that.

It had distracted him from *everything.*

Normally, Gael took after his dad in the anxiety department—he always seemed to be worrying about something: whether he was taking the right number of AP classes; whether he was practicing his tenor sax enough; whether

18

his little sister, Piper, would ever make friends her own age (she was just so smart and so uninterested in normal eight-year-old things); whether the occasional constellation of zits on his forehead made him wholly undateable. And on and on and on.

But when he and Anika had finally started dating, it was like none of the stressful things mattered. Because even though it was arguably at the worst time of his life, even though it had only been just over a month since his parents had broken the still-difficult-to-comprehend news, he suddenly felt . . . good.

His family might be falling apart, but Gael and Anika were just beginning.

And now she'd dumped him.

And he was somehow supposed to believe that it was all because of *Mason?* Mason, who'd been raiding their freezer for Bagel Bites since they were both Piper's age. Mason, who routinely accompanied Gael to indie movies even though he was an action-and-shitty-dialogue sort of guy.

Mason, who knew more than anyone how much his parents' split had hurt him.

"Gael?"

"Everything is fine," he stammered, scowling at the floor.

"What was going on between you and Anika?"

"We were just talking." He spoke the words slowly. If he said too much, he'd lose it.

"One sec," Mrs. Channing said. She shuffled through the chaos of her desk—stacks of papers, two empty coffee cups patterned with caked lipstick. It was nice how Anika wore gloss instead, Gael thought automatically, before pushing it quickly away.

Mrs. Channing opened her file cabinet, flipped through the bloated folders, then pushed two pamphlets across the desk.

Pamphlet #1
Breaking Up and Breaking Down:
Coping with the Highs and Lows
of High School Romance

Pamphlet #2
No Means No: A Primer on
Relationships and Consent

Gael stared in disbelief. "My mom's a women's studies professor at UNC," he told her. "I know all about that no-means-no stuff. I just wanted to talk. She's my girlfriend."

Mrs. Channing took a deep breath. "I know it's hard, Gael, but it didn't look like Anika wanted to talk."

Mrs. Channing didn't get it. Gael was the ultimate respecter of women. He never ogled girls like Mason did, that shithead. He loved Anika.

"Can I please go?" he asked. His voice cracked, midsentence.

"Yes." She scribbled a note for his teacher and set it on top of the pamphlets. "Off to class."

Gael grabbed the stack and moved for the door.

"Oh, and Gael," she called.

"Yeah?"

"It happens to all of us."

"What?"

"A broken heart."

I watched in agony as Gael stomped out of her office, wadded up the papers in his hand—note for his teacher and all—tossed them into the trash, pushed through the front door of the building, and stepped out into the sun.

the second-worst day
of gael's life, continued

GAEL SPENT THE REST OF THE DAY HIDING OUT IN HIS CAR in the school parking lot, eating a half-full bag of stale chips he'd found in the glove compartment, moping as he flipped through fuzzy radio stations, and angrily picking off the crumpled petals of the stupid $6.99 bunch of carnations until the flowers were all destroyed.

Gael had nowhere else to wallow. His mom was home, since she didn't teach her first class until 2:00 P.M., and she had a great bullshit detector. And the thought of sitting alone in his dad's dingy apartment was even more depressing than this.

As the hours rolled by, the faint buzz of each period's bell drifted through the parking lot. Gael tried his best not to think about anything at all, but it was no use. He imagined Anika and Mason, sitting close in the cafeteria, their bodies touching as she ate sour-cream-and-onion Pringles, Mason shoving that gross rectangular cafeteria pizza into his mouth. He saw his classmates laughing as they spread the news that Gael had finally found out. His high school was just small enough that everyone knew everyone's business, popular or not.

He saw himself, shocked and shamed and trailing after the guidance counselor, the school's official recipient of pity.

Worse, he saw the truth, bold and blaring like the old-timey marquee at the Varsity Theater on Franklin: Anika wasn't his anymore. Anika was hooking up with Mason now.

Anika, his *girlfriend*, was hooking up with the guy he'd known since he was seven: the guy who, in fourth grade, had suffered through two weeks without recess for punching a kid who'd called Gael a dork; the guy who frequently said that as adults, he and Gael would marry twin models, buy houses next door to each other, and have an obscenely large home theater system for Gael's movies and Mason's video games.

That guy.

By the time 3:15 rolled around and the school's final bell rang, students eagerly flooding the parking lot, Gael's sadness had morphed into full-fledged anger. Before he could change his mind, he whipped the car door open and slammed it bitterly behind him, heading as quickly as he could to the band room.

High school marching band was its own little microcosm of the world. More a study in sociology than in woodwinds and brass: There were the band geeks, pimply and a tad too greasy, making out with one another every chance they got. There were the no-nonsense go-getters, eager to fill a line on their college applications, marching without rhythm or passion. There was the percussion section, hipsters-to-be whose arms would be full of tattoos in a few years' time. And there were the tuba players, chunky and asexual, as if they were slowly morphing into their instrument of choice.

Gael had always thought of himself and Anika and Mason as separate from these stereotypes. Mason was a blue-eyed drummer, sure, but he still spent most of his time with Gael and Anika. Gael joined because his love of old movies had led to a love of movie soundtracks and a love of tenor sax. And Anika was different from Amberleigh Shotwell's harem of mean-girl flute players, with their sheets of long hair forming a shiny wall that said, Don't talk to us. We shouldn't even be in marching band. Anika would never make someone feel like she didn't want them around, in band or otherwise. She always knew how to fill the space between people, instantly putting them at ease, whether through obsessively quoting Firefly or by complimenting them in genuine, unique ways, like when she'd told Jenna her new bangs made her look like a "posh librarian." Anika made people feel like they mattered.

It was one of the many reasons Gael had fallen for her. Why he felt that their love was actually real. He and Anika had been a legit band couple, sure, but they weren't the same as those greasy PDA-mongers in front of their instrument lockers before practice. Their relationship was classy, like a Wes Anderson movie, or a Mumford & Sons song, the kind of love you couldn't scoff at. The kind of love he never imagined could go away.

And now apparently it already had.

(I can't help but interject here. Everyone thinks their romance is classy AF. No one sits there comparing their coupledom to the stuff of Lifetime movies. And no one thinks it will go away because, if you did, you'd never take a chance. Luckily, the human heart is not that logical.)

Gael walked over to where his sax was stored. Nearby, Amberleigh made a sad face, looking at him with her bottom lip puffed out.

"Have you seen Mason?" he asked.

Amberleigh shook her head, and he turned away before she could deliver any more pity. Practice didn't officially start until 3:30. Most kids used the fifteen minutes beforehand to talk with friends, but sometimes, Gael and Anika had gone to her car and held hands across the bucket seats, his thumb circling hers in a kind of dance that was more erotic than the crap Mason watched on his laptop. They'd blast classic rock, lean the seats way back, and just look at each other . . .

The vision disappeared instantly as Anika and Mason walked into the band room together, hand in freaking hand.

Their faces looked surprised, and for a second, Gael thought they'd turn away, but Anika seemed determined not to avoid him. She let go of Mason's hand and plastered on the stupidest, fakest smile. Mason trailed behind her.

"Uhh, hey," she said. "I didn't see you in English."

"Hey?" Gael asked. "All you have to say is '*hey*'?"

Anika bit her lip. "I guess this is a little awkward. I know you want to talk. I just wanted to wait until you'd calmed down . . ."

"And you think I'm calm *now*?" Gael yelled. The band room was almost full, though Mr. Potter hadn't arrived. Everyone was staring, but Gael didn't care. He turned to Anika. "You cheated on me with my *best friend*."

Anika's eyes got watery. She looked at Mason, but his eyes shifted quickly around the room, then down to his oversized feet, avoiding both of them.

That didn't stop Gael from saying what he had to. He turned to Mason. "And you just abandoned the entire bro code for a hook up? You could have any girl you wanted! Why did it have to be *my girlfriend*?"

Mason sighed but didn't look up to face him.

Anika dabbed at the corner of her eye but at least had the decency to look at him. She sniffled. "We just want you to know that your friendship is really important to us, Gael."

Us.

Us?

Us!!?&!!?@%!!?

Gael's hands drew into fists at his sides, and his stomach clenched. Being cheated on was bad enough, but the two of them didn't even show an ounce of genuine remorse.

Then, before he realized what he was doing, Gael punched his former best friend with all his might—straight in his stupid face, the one girls always seemed to find so endearing. Mason fell back into a mishmash of music stands, breaking his fall, clanking dramatically as they fell to the ground.

Gael's eyes were on the verge of tears, his body hot, his head throbbing. He vaguely sensed lots of yelling and people rushing around him, but he could hardly tell what was going on.

Gael ran, and he didn't stop until he was out of the band room, in the daylight, and far enough from school so no one could see.

His breathing got heavy as awful visions filled his head—Mason holding Anika's hand, kissing her lips, hugging her, undressing her, laughing with her, smiling with her, having everything with her that Gael would never, ever have again.

throwback to the best day of gael's life

FOR GAEL, IT HADN'T BEEN HARD TO CHOOSE THE DAY TO Beat All Days.

It had been one of those weirdly cool afternoons in August, the last Saturday before the start of senior year. Nothing to do but waste time and luxuriate in the final weekend of summer.

Since June, he and the usual suspects had spent most Saturdays at Jenna Carey's. Jenna was Anika's longtime BFF, and she had a pool. But this Saturday, it had been too cold for swimming. Gael thought about that sometimes, how if it had been ninety degrees, they'd have gone to Jenna's pool, and maybe he and Anika never would have become he and Anika.

They didn't go to Jenna's that day—instead, everyone walked down Franklin Street to load up on donuts at Krispy Kreme.

Franklin was a mishmash of bookstores, yummy food (late night and otherwise), and shops hawking everything from thrifty hipster wares to UNC gear to preppy woven belts that the frat boys always wore. Historic buildings and brick sidewalks gave it that throwback downtown feel, while music joints, tattoo shops, and seedy bars reminded you that it was, indeed, a college drag.

They parked themselves on the steps of the Chapel Hill post office, which offered a perfect view of the UNC campus, with its columned brick buildings, sweeping lawns, and masses of trees whose leaves had yet to turn. It was the kind of campus you saw in TV shows about college, the kind that made you want to wear a sweatshirt with felt letters.

When they were done with their donuts and had gotten most of the flaky sugar off their lips, Anika asked if anyone wanted to go to the "Life of a Star" show at the Morehead Planetarium, which was just across the street.

One by one, everyone bailed. Mason said he had to head to his grandmother's for an early dinner; Jenna said paying to look at fake stars sounded "next-level boring"; and Danny Lee, who was Gael's best friend besides Mason and who'd recently started dating Jenna, nodded in new-boyfriend agreement. Gael—who, despite following IFLScience on Facebook, did not really know much about a star's life span or about science in general—still knew better than to pass up a precious hour and a half alone with Anika and said, "Sure."

When it was just the two of them, Gael and Anika headed toward the planetarium, walking past the bench nestled under a towering oak tree where, legend had it, if you shared a kiss, it meant you were destined to get married.

(Fun fact: Most people who kiss on that bench do *not* get married. I would know.)

The planetarium was all domed and majestic like

something out of a movie; Gael hadn't been there since he was a kid on a field trip. A sign outside said the next show was at 3:30. They were just in time, one of the many factors that fell in his favor that day. When the box office girl asked, "Y'all together?" Gael awkwardly said "yes" before either of them had a chance to really think about it.

Rows of tightly packed seats lined the walls of the circular room, and they chose two in the back. The tiny seats were smaller than the ones on an airplane, the kind that press you up against the person sitting next to you.

And then the show started and the stars came out, thousands of them, more than you ever saw in real life, even in places like Wyoming, where Gael had once been. It was like they were in a giant, turned-over pasta strainer, with countless tiny openings letting in spots of light just for them.

Gael could hear Anika breathing, but he couldn't see her. When he turned his head to try, there was only blackness.

And then the most amazing thing happened, something he never could have planned, the kind of thing Gregory Peck might execute flawlessly, but not him, not Gael Brennan. (I have to say that I love that about my job: watching ordinary guys become romantic heroes, just for a moment or two.) Gael set his hand on the armrest between them, but Anika's was already there. His first instinct was to pull back, but before he could, Anika flipped her hand over, and her long, graceful fingers wove between his and squeezed.

The stars disappeared and there was a seductive glow as the ceiling displayed an image of a mammoth red supergiant.

Gael turned to Anika. He could see her now, her face cast with red, and she was looking right at him.

By the time their lips touched, it was black again.

When the show ended and they stepped outside, into the blinding light of the late afternoon, Gael assumed the whole thing would be forgotten. Making out with your crush in the dark was part of a separate universe, a fluke—perhaps it was something Anika wanted to check off her bucket list. (Which wasn't *that* crazy of a thought. Anika was an Adventurer[2] when it came to romance.)

But she turned to him, her lip gloss smeared, her cheeks flushed. "Want to go to Cosmic?" she asked.

---

2. Adventurer: One who primarily seeks out a partner for life's adventures (and misadventures), and who doesn't feel the need for overly romantic gestures, saccharine phrases, or deep discussions about the future. May result in downplaying more serious emotions or situations in favor of "just seeing where it goes." May also result in a fun, fly-by-the-seat-of-your-pants relationship that keeps both partners excited and fulfilled.

Besides Spanky's, Cosmic was Gael's favorite restaurant on Franklin, if you could call it a proper restaurant. The full name was Cosmic Cantina, but when your food was served in a Styrofoam box, it seemed a little silly to use the full name. "The super burrito is calling me," Anika added.

"Sounds great," Gael said, and he held her hand again as they walked back onto Franklin Street, toward the lure of greasy burritos and nachos. In the course of one planetarium show, they'd gone from band hangout buddies to so much more.

Anika always got what she wanted, whether it was free guacamole on her Cosmic burrito or extra credit on her math test.

Now, suddenly, she wanted him.

It made Gael feel both amazing and totally out of control.

(Worth noting: Everyone gets scared by that out-of-control feeling. And I do mean *everyone*.)

Anika's hand in his felt natural, and the energy between them felt big and important, straight-up literary, like Tristan and Isolde. Cathy and Heathcliff. Romeo and Juliet.

But the thing that Gael forgot to remember was that, whether the author is Shakespeare, Emily Brontë, or whoever the hell wrote *Tristan and Isolde*, all of those stories have one thing in common:

They end badly.

la vie en woes

"YOU'RE HOME EARLY AGAIN." SAMMY, PIPER'S INCREDIBLY annoying babysitter, adjusted her thick, rectangular glasses. "I thought you had all kinds of extracurriculars and stuff?"

It was Monday, almost a week since the breakup, and Sammy and his little sister were perched in the dining room, as was their habit. Piper didn't even look up from her *Elementary French* book. "He's supposed to be in marching band, but he's skipped *cinq fois*, counting today." She didn't wait for Gael to ask. "That means five times."

Sammy smirked. "Suddenly don't like playing 'YMCA' in formation anymore?"

"I don't want to talk about it," Gael said.

"Why not?" Sammy leaned her elbow on the table and rested her chin on her hand.

"Forgive me if I don't want to tell all my life problems to my little sister and her babysitter," Gael snapped.

"Hey," Piper protested, her short light brown hair swinging back and forth as she shook her head. "She's not my babysitter." Indignation was written plainly across her eight-and-three-quarters-year-old face. "I told *you* she's my French tutor."

Gael couldn't help but laugh. Sammy had been babysitting Piper after school since Gael started marching band his sophomore year, but last August, when his parents found out that Sammy would be majoring in French when she started at UNC, they offered to pay her more if French lessons were involved. Now Pipes absolutely abhorred the word *babysitter*.

Sammy fiddled with a page of her *Candide* and tipped back in the fancy dining room chair to look him in the eye. "So you're really not going to tell us why you're skipping?"

Gael swore that Sammy hadn't always been this annoying. They'd always been friendly before. When Gael arrived home, Sammy would ask him a few questions about school and friends and the like, then quickly go back to whatever book she was reading, her eyes jutting across the page behind frameless glasses while she waited for his mom to get home with her check.

But since she'd started at UNC, she'd chopped off her hair, dyed it dark chocolaty brown, replaced the mom glasses with those of the nerdy-but-still-very-cool variety, and talked incessantly of annoying things like French writers and the "prison-industrial complex." His mom ate it up, but Gael found her sudden snobbery a bit . . . fake.

Of course, Sammy had become a lot more annoying now that Gael was coming home earlier. He was forced into daily interactions with an uppity French lit major who thought it was her job to not only take care of his sister but to pry into his life. This hadn't been a problem until

The Ultimate Betrayal. Otherwise known as the Loss of Girlfriend and Best Friend in One. Basically, the end of life as Gael had known it.

(I know, Romantics are *such* drama queens.)

"You can't skip something that you quit," Gael said finally.

"Do your parents know you quit?" Sammy asked. Lately, it seemed like Sammy could go on asking questions forever and ever and ever. It was no wonder she and Piper got along so well.

"Why does it matter to you?"

"They have no idea," Piper chimed in, closing her book and staring at him accusingly with her wide green eyes. She perched her chin on her hand, imitating Sammy's gesture.

"Are you okay, though?" Sammy asked, her voice a tad softer. "You don't seem like the type to just quit things."

"I'm fine," he muttered, avoiding Sammy's eyes. "Now can you just leave me alone?"

Sammy and Piper exchanged identical looks. They made an odd pair—the lanky college hipster and her miniature bespectacled minion. Mercifully, they didn't say anything more.

True to his new routine, Gael headed for the kitchen pantry and straight to the chocolate stash, which included a trove of fun-size Snickers bars that Anika used to raid. Since the breakup, he'd already discreetly replaced the bag twice. He grabbed three, shoved them into his pockets, and headed to his room without glancing back at Sammy or Piper.

Back in his cave, Gael closed the curtains that his mom opened every morning and popped a movie he'd seen too many times to count into the Blu-ray player. He unwrapped the first Snickers bar, letting himself forget the past week for just a moment; the crinkly coated paper made a strangely comforting sound, even if the taste of the candy reminded him bittersweetly of Anika's kiss.

Gael was a mess of emotions. Sometimes he felt like Anika was dead, like she'd been replaced by some kind of lookalike robot like in *The Stepford Wives*—the original one, not the shitty remake. Sometimes he felt like *he* was dead, like all his insides had been erased, leaving only numbness and emptiness. Sometimes he wanted to call Anika and scream. Sometimes he wanted to beat the shit out of Mason, even though his knuckles were still sore from that band-room punch.

But all the time, no matter what crazy thoughts took over his head, he really just wanted to disappear. To slowly eat his chocolate and melt into the bed. He realized in horror that even his coping method was pathetic, straight out of a girly romantic comedy. He *hated* romantic comedies.

Gael took another bite of chocolate.

(Another fun fact: Chocolate actually does make you feel better after a breakup, due to the presence of phenylethylamine, the chemical your brain releases when you fall in love.)

The couple of hours before his mom got home was the only time that Gael didn't have to pretend to be pulled together. He couldn't bring himself to lose it in front of her. He'd done enough of that last summer, after his parents broke the utterly confounding news. His mom had alternated between breaking down herself and inviting him to her power yoga classes.

Not that weekends at his dad's were any better. Since the separation, his father had begged Gael to join him on his daily four-mile runs—and a family therapy session or two. If his dad knew that Gael's own romance had fallen apart, he would almost certainly insist upon it. He'd pass, *thanks*.

Gael turned down the TV and closed his eyes, hoping against hope to drift quickly to sleep, aka oblivion.

Every day since TUB (The Ultimate Betrayal) had been a disaster. He had English with Anika, who never failed to shoot him a forced smile. Then chemistry with Mason, where they were *lab partners*. Gael refused to talk to either of them. In the past week, he'd barely exchanged words with anyone.

Things were even awkward with Danny. Even though he was Gael's best friend besides Mason, the dude was gaga for Jenna, and Jenna had long been Anika's BFF. As such, this had become the unspoken rule among them: Jenna was Team Anika, Danny was Team Jenna, and by the transitive property, Danny couldn't be on Gael's side.

Gael hadn't ever thought to make friends outside of their little group. He hadn't hedged his bets, if you will.

He'd put all his eggs in one basket.

And those eggs had decided to hook up with each other behind his back.

in which i witness the unraveling of gael and mason's bromance

IT'S NOT LIKE I DIDN'T HAVE A PLAN FOR GAEL. I DID—
believe me on this one.

It's just that certain circumstances (yes, including some of my own doing) had made my plan that much more difficult to implement. Not impossible, of course, just . . . tricky. I am very good at my job. At least I *was* very good at my job before this untimely oversight. But I digress.

Allow me to introduce a not-uncommon but wholly unpleasant part of the gig: the undoing of friendships. Many have ended over me, or a perception of me, and it always seems so unnecessary. I want to shake people, remind them of the time, not long before, when they were each other's favorite.

Anyway, back to Gael and Mason. Not only was the end of their bromance devastating, it was straight-up dangerous. See, real friendship is its own kind of love, which means it comes with its own kind of heartbreak—and Gael had had more than his fair share lately.

Between his parents' split, Anika's betrayal, and

Mason's involvement, Gael was rocking a triple-whammy of heartbreak.

Which made the following scene, the Friday after the breakup, only that much more difficult to watch:

"You can't just sit there and not talk to me all period," Mason said.

Gael didn't look up. He traced over his chemistry notes in pen, eyes flitting occasionally to the eyewash station. He spent a good portion of every period plotting out chemistry-related methods to maim his former best friend.

"Uhh, dude?"

"What?" Gael snapped.

Mason took a deep breath. "I said, 'You can't just—'"

"I know!" Gael said. "I heard you. I'm not deaf. I don't want to talk to you."

"But we're lab partners. We have to, like, talk about measurements and stuff."

(It's worth noting here that, as per usual, Mason was wholly unaware of the assignment while Gael did all of the work.)

"Yeah, and we *used* to be best friends," Gael said.

Mason put his big hands on the table, squeezing the edge until his knuckles were white. "Are you really going to throw away like a decade of friendship over what happened with me and Anika?"

Gael looked him in the eyes for once. *What happened.* Like the two of them had accidentally broken his Blu-ray player or something. "You're the one who threw the friendship away by sneaking around with Anika for a *week* before I found out. Not me."

Mason ran a hand through his curly hair and fiddled with the chemistry book he almost never opened, avoiding Gael's eyes. "I'm sorry," He said. "It just kind of . . . happened. She—"

Gael held up his hand. "I don't want to hear the details, okay?" He shook his head vehemently. "I *loved* her."

Mason's eyes finally met Gael's. "You never told me that."

Gael crossed his arms. "Because I thought you'd make fun of me."

Mason laughed, but it was a sad kind of laugh, a weak one. "I probably would have made fun of you for falling in love after a couple of months," he said.

"Well—*news flash*—you can love someone in two months," Gael said.

(He's right on this one, of course. You can love someone in two minutes. I've seen two seconds, on rare occasions.)

"I don't mean to be a dick," Mason said carefully.

Too late, Gael thought.

"But did she love you?" Mason continued. "Like, did she ever say it?"

Gael pressed his lips together.

Mason raised his eyebrows, tilted his head. While he waited for an answer, he drummed a beat on the table.

"It doesn't matter," Gael spit out. "It doesn't change what you did."

Mason stopped drumming. "I know what I did was shitty, but I'm just saying I've crushed on the Chili's waitress longer than you and Anika were ever going out."

(As much as I consider myself fully Team Gael in this situation, this was not entirely Mason's fault. He didn't understand what—frankly—no one in the world fully understands besides Gael and me: that no matter if it was or wasn't the real thing, for Gael, it was everything.)

"You're an asshat," Gael said.

And without another word, Gael went back to plotting chemistry-lab attack methods.

sleepless in chapel hill

NOW LET US RETURN TO GAEL IN HIS COCOON OF DESPAIR.

Our reluctant hero was almost asleep when he heard a loud knock on the door.

Before Gael could speak, Piper burst in. He looked at the clock on his phone—despite his requests to be left alone, his little sister had given him less than a half an hour of Gael-time before her grand entrance. Apparently, *Elementary French* was done for the day.

"It's dark in here," she observed.

Knowing that he would certainly be unable to drift off now, he paused the movie and unwrapped another Snickers bar. "That's kind of the point."

She flipped the light on, blinding him. "Are you going to be in a bad mood on your birthday, too? Because we never go to sushi anymore, and you better not ruin it."

His birthday. It was this Friday, and his mom had planned this stupid family dinner at his favorite sushi place. Gael could hardly stomach the thought of eating raw fish with his dad conspicuously absent and pretending it was all okay. He took another bite of Snickers.

(Side note: Pre-birthday breakups are *the worst*. Right along with pre-Christmas, pre–Valentine's Day, and pre-anniversary.)

"Don't you have some verbs to conjugate?" Gael asked, changing the subject, as Piper perched on his bed.

She shook her head.

"Will you just leave me alone?" he asked. "Please?"

"You have chocolate in your teeth," she told him.

He shoved the last Snickers in, answering his little sister with his mouth full. "Now I have more."

Sammy appeared and leaned against the doorway. "Sexy."

Gael rolled his eyes and chewed intentionally slowly, which wasn't very hard between all the peanuts and caramel and chocolate. Sammy just stood there, arms crossed, shaking her head.

"What do you want, anyway?" he asked. "I was trying to go to sleep."

"Your little sister wanted to make sure you were okay." She tilted her head to the side and gave him a careful smile, and for a second, she looked like the old Sammy, before the cool glasses and big ideas. It's not like they'd been great friends, but she'd been far less annoying, at least.

He still didn't want to talk to her.

"I'm not," he said. "Okay? Which should be pretty clear. But now you both have an official answer."

"Come on, Pipes," Sammy said. "Let's get through the rest of your French chapter."

Piper hopped off the bed like an obedient puppy. Sammy put a hand on Piper's shoulder and knelt down to her level. "Start the next exercise. I'll be there in a sec."

Sammy waited until Piper was down the hall to talk. "You know you can't go on just wallowing in your misery forever."

"Jesus," Gael said. "You're not *my* babysitter."

Sammy put a hand on her hip like she always did when she was making a point. "I'm just saying. You have to move on, pull yourself out of it. It's the only way."

"Why do you even care?" he muttered, as he watched the blades of the ceiling fan whir.

"I'm keen on continuing to earn my fifteen bucks an hour, which I'm guessing your mom won't be so into paying if she knows you're sitting here at home every afternoon."

Gael couldn't care less about Sammy's fifteen an hour. "That's really helpful coming from you, with your—what— three-year relationship going strong?"

Sammy drew a quick breath. I could see all the hurt, which was still so fresh, come rushing back. Then her face hardened, and her answer came out harsh: "My relationship has nothing to do with you, okay?"

"I'm just saying, unless you've been dumped out of the blue, you don't get it."

She laughed. Only I could see that she really wanted to cry. Then Sammy repeated the mantra she'd been saying to herself for the last month and a half.

"*Si vous vous sentez seul quand vous êtes seul, vous êtes en mauvaise compagnie.*" She said it slowly, her voice all nasally and French.

(Her accent was actually pretty impressive, not that Gael cared about that.)

"And what's that supposed to mean?" Gael asked. He had a feeling it was a dig of some sort, knowing Sammy.

"It's Jean-Paul Sartre," she said. "Look it up."

And with that, she flipped the lights off, turned on her heel, and pulled the door shut behind her.

It took him ten full minutes of Googling before he found the translation.

If you are lonely when you're alone, you are in bad company.

Which only led him to one conclusion:

Jean-Paul Sartre, like Sammy Sutton, had never had a broken heart.

eighteen candles

THAT FRIDAY EVENING, HIS MOM KNOCKED ON HIS DOOR and poked her head in. "You all set?"

Gael sat up in his bed, where he'd been lying down, staring at the ceiling, and wishing he didn't have to go to his stupid birthday dinner.

As torturous as the thought of ringing in the big one-eight with a sad, three-person dinner was, so was the thought of disappointing his mom. "All right, all right," Gael said reluctantly. He pulled on his Chucks, squeezing his feet in without messing with the laces.

His mom walked in the room and leaned against his closet door. Her dark, almost-black hair was pulled into a bun, and she was wearing a black dress with a scarf she'd knitted herself, along with these dangly turquoise earrings that Gael and his dad had picked out a couple of birthdays ago. "I just spoke to your dad, actually. He's going to come, too."

Gael raised his eyebrows. "I thought you said we were going to do stuff separately."

"Well, I changed my mind, okay?" Immediately, she forced a smile, as if surprised at herself. Angela Brennan, who made her living raising her voice to young college

47

students, entreating them to open their eyes to the bullshit of the system, was a beacon of cheerfulness at home. He'd gone with his dad to pick her up once, and they'd caught the tail-end of her lecture—it had been crazy to see the petite woman who cut the crusts off his bread talking vehemently about housework being the "second shift."

Of course, only now could he really see that her cheerfulness took work. Now that his dad was gone, she was constantly trying to hold it together—Gael wondered sometimes how long she'd been doing that before his dad left.

(A long time, actually. Longer than even I had realized.)

She took a deep breath and clasped her hands together. "I just meant, I know this has all been very hard for you, and so I thought, in the transition, that it would be nice to do something as a family." Her smile fell flat as she waited for his reaction.

Gael just shrugged. "Whatever."

Her smile came back in full force. "Oh, by the way," she said as she moved toward the door. "I ran into Sammy on campus this morning. I asked her to come, too. We'll pick her up on the way."

Another shrug. "I honestly don't care who comes, Mom."

She tilted her head to the side, smirking. "Whatever you say . . ."

The truth was, all Gael wanted was to binge-eat cake and Snickers and watch anywhere from two to ten movies.

But he guessed he should be used to not getting what he wanted by now.

* * * * *

It was dim inside the sushi place, which was decorated to make you forget you were eating raw fish nearly three hours from the ocean, with earthy colors and paper shades and potted curlicue bamboo plants and waiters wearing all black. Sizzling sounds came from the kitchen, and the place smelled salty and delicious.

Even though they arrived early, Gael's dad had beaten them there and was sitting at a big table in the middle. Arthur Brennan was passionate about four things in life: running, Russian history, UNC basketball, and punctuality.

His dad, easily the tallest person in the room, stood up as they walked in and shifted his weight from foot to foot while nervously running a hand through his meticulously cut and parted sandy blond hair. His dad and his mom proceeded to do an awkward dance of deciding whether to hug (they didn't) and where to sit (Piper and Sammy ended up taking two spots between them so they didn't have to be *too* close). Gael took a seat next to his mom, and it didn't take him long to realize there were two extra seats, right next to him.

"What's with the chairs?" he asked.

And then—

"Anika!" His mom stood up, and Gael turned around,

already feeling ill, but it wasn't just Anika. It was Mason, too. Both walked in all smiling, like they hadn't just mutually broken his heart and ruined his life.

Gael forced his mouth into a smile as Sammy caught his eyes, her teeth clenched awkwardly, a look of pity creeping its way across her face.

Gael felt his body tense as Anika gave him a hug. "Happy birthday," she whispered, and she smelled like she always did, like coconut shampoo. She pulled back way too fast and yet not soon enough.

Then Mason suddenly clapped him on the back, saying, "Happy birthday, bro. I wasn't sure if I should show up or whatever, but when your mom called to make sure I was still coming, I was pumped."

"My mom?"

"She arranged the whole thing, dude."

The two of them quickly sat down, Anika sandwiched awkwardly between Gael and Mason. Gael wanted to explain that his mom had no idea what had happened between them—and that any calls from her absolutely did *not* have his blessing—but he couldn't exactly say anything with everyone there at the table.

(Just so everyone's clear on this, Anika and Mason showing up was about the last thing I wanted to happen at this juncture. I did my best to prevent them from coming—I tried to lure Mason to change his plans with a glimpse of a blockbuster action movie poster on the drive home from school, and Anika even had some, ahem, mysterious car trouble. But it was no use. Anika's mom is a whiz with cars, and Mason cared far more about potentially healing his friendship with Gael than any movie, no matter how many car chases it promised.)

For Gael, the minutes stretched by endlessly, as his dad began to get anxious about whether the waiter had forgotten about their appetizers. As his mom made a show of unfolding and refolding her napkin and trying to avoid his dad's eyes. As Piper looked just a touch too happy, probably naïvely hoping that after one joint dinner his parents would actually make up. As Mason made a totally Mason comment about how it was good to see Mr. and Mrs. Brennan together again, and his parents scrambled to say how they had such a good friendship, and it was all going well, and blah blah blah. As Anika caught his eyes, and delivered a compassionate glance that only made him fume inside. If she was really so sorry about what had happened with his parents, she wouldn't have destroyed him like she did.

After another agonizing few minutes of placing their orders, his parents fumbling because they always got the "Sushi for Two" special, Anika fiddled in her bag and pulled out a cellophane-wrapped Blu-ray. "I wanted to give you this," she said quietly.

He stared at her, shocked. "A birthday present?" he whispered angrily. "I don't want anything from you."

"Just take it," she said. "I had to order it special."

She shoved it into his hands and smiled.

"What's that?" his mom asked.

"Nothing," he said.

"*Vertigo!*" his mom said. "I introduced this to you, Gael, remember?"

"I know, Mom," he said.

She took it out of his hands. "Deluxe edition and everything. What a thoughtful gift. Is this from you, Anika?"

"Yes, Mrs. Brennan," Anika said sweetly. She sounded so fake. Had she always sounded so fake? Gael wondered.

"Well, you sure know Gael, I'll say that much," his mom said. "He *loves* old movies. Unlike Arthur."

In the past, his dad would have responded by delivering an impassioned argument about why new movies were so much better than old ones, but his parents didn't have those types of playful discussions anymore. His dad just shrugged.

"I never watched any Hitchcock before Gael got me into it," Anika said. Her voice was super high-pitched, about an octave higher than normal. Mason, for his part, was staring at his fork, avoiding everyone.

"It's not that amazing to buy a movie," Gael said. "One click on Amazon. Boom. Anyone could do it."

His mom gasped. "Gael. I think it was a very thoughtful gift from your girlfriend."

"She's not my girlfriend," he spat.

Everyone went quiet, looking at him like he'd just farted, including perfect little gift-giving Anika. She stared at him like this was somehow his fault.

Gael didn't want to do this here, not in front of his

family—and Mason and Sammy and the whole freaking restaurant—but he couldn't stop. "You seriously think a stupid gift will fix everything?"

"Gael, stop." Anika's eyes started to well with tears. "Don't do this."

Gael threw his hands into the air. "It's not even from the Criterion Collection!"

"They don't have *Vertigo* in Criterion," Anika said meekly.

"Well, if you really knew me, you'd know I'd have wanted to wait until it comes out in Criterion," he said, his voice fully a yell now.

"Hey, come on, dude," Mason said, placing a hand on the back of Anika's chair.

Anika didn't look at Mason. Instead, she closed her mouth and put on her saddest, feel-bad-for-me eyes and said: "I'm sorry. I didn't think—"

"Of course you didn't. You two only think about yourselves."

Gael turned to face his audience. "Guess what, family? Since we're all here together, watching me have a total breakdown, you might as well know that she cheated on me! With him!" He pointed to Mason.

For the briefest of moments, Gael saw a look of shock pass across his dad's face—or was it actually guilt? Gael paused. His parents had never given him a reason for why they'd split, and over the past couple of weeks, Gael had started to wonder if it might be his dad's fault. His dad had taken to running into his bedroom when his phone rang, answering with the door firmly shut, almost like he had something to hide. Maybe his own father was no better than Mason or Anika.

But he didn't have time to figure it out. Because that's when the waiter came out with a caterpillar roll with a lit candle in it, a group of people around him, singing in Japanese to the tune of the "Happy Birthday" song.

(I'd tried to delay this: In the kitchen, the candle went out no fewer than four times due to a mysteriously over-active exhaust fan, but unfortunately, all the waiters had lighters in their pockets.)

Gael pushed his chair back and jumped up before anyone could stop him. He tried to avoid the eyes of his parents and Sammy and his little sister, but it was impossible not to see the shock and confusion on their faces. He attempted to make a break for it, but the waiters had surrounded him, their chanting morphing from the birthday song into "Make a wish! Make a wish!"

Gael glared down at the celebratory sushi roll in front of him. "Fine, sure. I'll make a wish." The waiters cut off their refrain, the restaurant suddenly unnaturally silent—other diners had finally caught on that something more interesting was happening than the average birthday party. But Gael was far past caring about making a scene. He squeezed his eyes shut, and with a big exhale, blew out the lone candle. He made a big show of opening his eyes and looking around the table expectantly.

"Nope," Gale pronounced. "You're all still here. Guess it didn't come true."

Then he pushed through the waiters and stormed out of the restaurant.

(I told you Romantics were dramatic.)

love and the art of relationship maintenance

AT THIS POINT IN THE NARRATIVE, I MIGHT AS WELL COME clean about my not-so-little mistake. In order for you to understand the gravity of the situation, I must delve ever so briefly into the past.

In the midnineties, I encouraged the romance of two young intellectual types in Chapel Hill, North Carolina. It was a good relationship, one in which I had utmost faith. These two were freaking *perfect* for each other.

I probably don't have to tell you this, but they were Gael's parents. One of my favorite success stories, to be honest.

And maybe that's where I went wrong. I was too confident. I got lazy.

The thing is, my work does not simply consist of getting people together. I also check in once every couple of years to see how it's going. Talk to any couple who's been together awhile, and they'll tell you that love ebbs and flows, that there are ups and downs.

What they don't know is that a lot of those ups have to do with me. Suddenly, they'll be flooded with memories of the good times, as tingly and fluttery as if these moments had only just happened. Or they'll be in the middle of an argument, and one of them will find the strength to be the bigger person, take the high road, and move beyond the fight.

My maintenance work is just that—maintenance. I can't save a relationship that's run its course. But when two people still have a lot of love for each other, I know just how to get them back on track.

Problem is, with Gael's parents, I missed my check-in. Actually, I missed *three* check-ins. I've been over it hundreds of times, and I still can't figure out quite how it happened.

Was it the slow but steady uptick in my work? (Thanks for nothing, Tinder.) Was it William and Kate's royal wedding? (You don't even want to know how many fires I have to put out when the *whole entire world* witnesses a romance and catches the love bug, many of them pursuing the wrong people as a result.) Was it simply a failure to update my mental calendar?

Nothing makes sense. I've dealt with encouraging love in difficult circumstances before (hello, cholera); it was not my first time tamping down an excess of emotion because two famous people got married; and my mental capabilities are far superior to iCal, trust me.

But whatever the reason, I messed up. Big time.

By the time I got my act together and did check in, it was too late. I could only watch as their marriage fell apart. Then I watched Gael (unsurprisingly) dive headfirst into a relationship with Anika in a desperate attempt to feel something other than sadness, to restore his own faith in love. And I watched her break his heart, as I knew she would.

Now I was watching Gael completely give up.

I couldn't just watch anymore. I had to step in more directly.

His future depended on it.

this is what i meant
about getting creative

GAEL HEADED ALONE DOWN EAST MAIN STREET, AND then continued along Franklin, trying to calm himself down and ignoring his mom's repeated phone calls. When he got to Franklin's main drag, he turned left into the alley that led to Rosemary Street. The flower lady was there, sitting in her usual spot: "Flowers, one dollar. Flowers, one dollar."

She lifted her head to look at Gael and pushed a rose at him. "For you."

Gael shook his head. "I don't have any cash," he said. "Sorry."

"It's free of charge." She pushed the flower at him again, her knobby knuckles powerful and insistent.

"It's okay," Gael said.

But she insisted. "Have a flower," she said again, shaking it in front of him like some kind of street evangelist.

He took it. "Thank you," he said.

"Whoever she is, she isn't worth it." Her wrinkled face looked serious, her eyes wide open like she didn't have a single doubt in the world that what she was saying was true. For a second, Gael wanted to ask her how she knew, how she could be so sure.

But then her gaze dropped from his, and she went back to arranging her flowers, calling out her typical refrain.

Gael continued down the alley, toward Rosemary Street, where he knew there would be far fewer people.

He walked down Rosemary, and after a few blocks, the acrid smell of spray paint tickled his nose. He turned. Against the brick wall of one of the dirtier dive bars were huge block letters, dripping as if freshly painted: *This, too, shall pass.*

He stopped, stared at the words, soaked them in for a second. Then he shook his head, kept walking. Inspirational shit works a lot better, he mused, when your whole life isn't already ruined.

In case you're wondering, I was not simply trying to perfect my tagging skills and give Banksy a run for his money. I was trying to reach Gael by any means possible: whether that meant urging old ladies to give away flowers or hand painting inspirational quotes. If I could only give him a tiny ray of hope, I could help him move past Anika and—eventually—on to Miss Right.

Of course, I hadn't anticipated a fatal flaw in my plan.

A dreaded enemy of True Love since the dawn of freaking time.

Ladies and gentleman, may I present my nemesis . . .

The Rebound.

it (accidentally)
happened one night

GAEL WAS ONLY A FEW MINUTES FROM HIS HOUSE, walking in the road to avoid a mess of spilled beer on the sidewalk, when a girl on a bike suddenly whirled toward him. The bike's front wheel hit his leg, his knees buckled, and he toppled forward, his hands rising to shield himself.

For a moment, he lay sprawled out on the sidewalk, clothes covered in the beer he'd been trying to avoid, and then he felt a hand touch his shoulder. "I'm so sorry."

Gael slowly rolled onto his side. Behind him, a black-and-red bike sat on top of a plastic takeout bag tied tightly shut. His flower was miraculously unhurt, stuck through the spokes of the front wheel like some kind of annoying metaphor for resilience.

Kneeling down next to him was a girl in a zip-up hoodie, Sriracha T-shirt, faded jeans, and Birkenstocks. Long, wispy blond hair peeked from beneath her bike helmet, which was covered with stickers of bands he'd never heard of. Her round cheeks were flushed red. "I can't believe I just did that," she said, her eyes getting all watery. "Are you okay?"

Gael pushed himself up to a sitting position and scooted onto the curb. "I'm all right, I think. What happened?"

"There was a cat," she said. "Darted right across the street in front of me. I swerved to miss it, but you were right there."

"Hit the human instead of the cat," he said caustically. "Nice."

Her face fell to a frown. "I really am sorry," she repeated.

Gael instantly felt bad. It wasn't enough that he'd publicly told his parents and Piper that he wished they'd all go away. Now he was snipping at random girls, too. Anika and Mason deserved it, sure, but the rest of the world? Not so much. He didn't want to sink to their level. He wondered if he had already.

Gael brushed the beery dirt off his shirt. "I was just kidding. I probably would have saved the kitty, too." His voice softened. "But you should look where you're going before you swerve. What if there had been a car? You could have been wiped out."

"I know." She bit her lip. "I had a biking accident recently. I'm all out of practice."

Gael ignored the ache in the back of his leg and the smell of beer emanating from the fibers of his T-shirt. "Eesh," he said. "An accident? That sucks. Were you okay?"

The girl smiled genuinely, and he had a deeply naïve thought, one that even he could tell was naïve: *She's not the kind of girl who'd cheat on her boyfriend.* "I'm fine, thanks. No bones broken, at least. But I guess I'm just a bit of a nervous rider now. I thought a quick ride to Cosmic would be no big deal, but I was wrong."

A girl who liked Cosmic *and* wouldn't cheat on him, he thought. Man, he had to stop this. Was he so messed up that he was projecting all his feelings onto the first girl he met?

(Yes, oh yes, he was. The Rebound is always a risk, but I hadn't worried too much about it with Gael given that he'd essentially become a social recluse. But now, one walk home alone, and I was already on the defensive. Not to mention, the Rebound in question was also a Meet Cute. You know, when two people run into each other out of the blue, and suddenly everyone thinks it's meant to be. Humans are experts at focusing so much on *how* they found someone over *who* that person actually is and *if* they're truly the right one. *Le sigh*.)

While Gael was debating whether it was totally cliché to crush on the first girl he met after Anika, his stomach growled as if unaware of his internal struggle.

"You got Cosmic?" he asked timidly.

The girl's gray eyes brightened. "You're a Cosmic fan?"

Gael smiled wide. "Isn't everyone? It's the best food on Franklin besides Spanky's, I-M-H-O."

"What do you order there?" she asked playfully, like this was some sort of challenge he had to pass.

Gael and Anika used to have drawn-out philosophical battles about what was better at Cosmic, nachos or burritos. The memory left with him with a visceral emptiness. And it wasn't just the hunger in his stomach.

"Nachos," he said. "And, yes, I realize that everyone else prefers the burritos."

"Well, it's your lucky day," she said. "Because I don't. You want some?"

Gael hesitated. He knew he should probably just go home, change his clothes, and take an Advil for the ache in his leg. He should apologize to his parents and be honest about what was going on with him. Hell, maybe he should even join his mom at a yoga class and, even crazier, tell his dad that a joint therapy session wasn't *that* horrible of an idea. Maybe they could even address his dad's secretive behavior.

But the thing was, he knew he wouldn't. He would watch more movies and eat more Snickers and take more unnecessary naps and continue to feel totally and completely shitty.

Plus, he thought, didn't he deserve this?

A nice, cute (if he was being totally honest) girl was offering him his favorite meal on his birthday. Sure, he didn't even know her name yet, but why not say yes?

"I really shouldn't take your food," he said, offering her an easy out if she wanted one.

"Please." Her face broke into a smile. "Cosmic is pretty paltry payment for being run down. And nachos are easy to share."

The girl stood up, lifted the bike, and retrieved the plastic bag underneath. She wheeled the bike out of the street, leaned it against the curb, and sat back down next to him.

"I'm Cara, by the way." She reached out her hand.

"I'm Gael." He shook hers in turn. "Do you live around here?"

"Yeah," she said. "Close by."

Gael stared at her. "I haven't seen you in school."

Cara smiled again. "I'm actually a freshman at UNC."

A nice, cute, *college freshman* who liked Cosmic. And unlike Sammy, a college freshman who didn't seem to be filled to the brim with big, pretentious ideas. Gael thought it was almost too good to be true.

"Anyway," Cara said. "Shall we see how our nachos held up in the crash?"

Our. He'd given up on ever being part of an "our" again.

Cara undid the bag's knot and pulled out a Styrofoam container dripping with black bean juice and watery salsa. She set it on her lap, evidently unperturbed by the idea of nachos getting on her jeans, and opened the top.

"Not horrible," she said, tilting the box toward him as a car full of frat guys passed by. "You approve?"

The box was a tornado of sour cream, grilled chicken,

white cheese, and beans, like the chips had decided to have a rager. "Looks good to me," he said.

"Just you wait," Cara said. She shuffled in the plastic bag and pulled out a dirty, half-used bottle of Valentina's.

"You stole the hot sauce?" Gael couldn't help himself. He burst out laughing.

"It was mostly empty," she said with a pout. "And I ran out the other night, and I keep forgetting to buy it . . . Do you mind?" She held the bottle over the nachos, midshake.

"No," Gael said. "Go ahead."

She doused everything in hot sauce, took a chip, and popped it in her mouth. "I love hot sauce," she said.

He nodded at her shirt. "I never would have guessed."

She laughed. "Yeah, I guess it's pretty obvious. Hot sauce is like my own personal rebellion. Both my parents hate everything spicy, whereas I'm all, can it be hot enough to make my tongue hurt, please?"

Gael laughed. "My dad thinks jalapeno peppers from the jar are like, explosion-level spicy. My mom's on my side, at least." They'd never have that argument again over dinner, he thought briefly, then pushed the thought away.

Cara popped another chip in her mouth.

"You probably think it's pathetic that hot sauce is my biggest rebellion, huh?"

Gael's mind instantly flashed to Anika's recent rebellion. He shook his head vehemently. He didn't need a girl who broke all the rules. He needed a girl who thought indulging in ultra-spicy hot sauce *was* breaking the rules.

"I don't think it's pathetic at all. Half the time, people just want to be assholes, so they call it rebellion. You know what I mean?"

She closed her mouth, swallowed, held his eyes. "I know exactly what you mean."

(I did, too. But just because Anika was wrong for him did not mean that this girl was right. Of course, convincing Gael of that would be another challenge altogether, that much was already clear.)

Gael didn't look away, and after a moment, Cara laughed nervously, broke his gaze, and grabbed another chip. "Me and rebellion just don't mix," she went on. "Even at school, everyone's all, let's go eye up frat boys with beer bellies every single weekend! And I'm like, I'm going to watch R-rated movies at home without having to feel awkward, and buy every kind of hot sauce ever!"

"I know," Gael said. He took a huge chip for himself. "I try and watch all the gory movies in my room in private. But my sister and mom pop in every five seconds, and my mom's a women's studies professor and she *hates* violence in movies, and it's so annoying. She starts shaking her head like it's me who's just whacked someone, not the dude onscreen."

Gael's tone was lighthearted, but he *had* wondered, lately: If he'd been more bold and exciting, more laid-back and carefree like Mason, would it have been enough for Anika? But that just wasn't Gael. He didn't want to get tanked every weekend and hook up with a ton of girls.

Maybe rebelling for him was nothing more than praying his mom wouldn't open the door too many times during a Tarantino movie. Did that mean he was doomed to be girlfriendless?

Almost as if responding to his thoughts, Cara held up a chip and tapped it against the one in Gael's hand. "To rebelling in little ways," she said. "And not asshole ones."

They laughed. And ate some more. Gael didn't talk about Anika, or his failed birthday dinner, or how he still didn't know why his parents split up, or his backstabbing best friend. They talked about Cara's current quest for the perfect pair of hiking boots, how annoying the college students on Franklin Street could be, and the bands on her helmet. For a few minutes, Gael felt kind of normal again.

When the box was empty, Cara shoved the trash into the plastic bag and stood up. "I should probably get going. I promised my friend I'd see a movie with her tonight."

Gael felt an instant sinking of his heart. This impromptu dinner had been like a reprieve from the epic disaster his life had become of late. He didn't want it to end.

"Okay." Gael stood up slowly. "Err, thanks for sharing your dinner with me." He paused. "It was nice to just randomly meet someone so cool."

He sounded lame. He knew it.

"Anytime," Cara said. "It was great to meet you, too. Sorry for hitting you with my bike."

"It's okay," Gael said. His leg was practically throbbing,

but he'd been so wrapped up in Cara, he'd forgotten about it until now. "Really."

Cara lifted up her bike. "Oh," she said. "I didn't even see your flower." She pulled it out of the spokes, not a petal harmed. "I hope I didn't make you late for a date or anything," she said, her voice rising just a touch at the end. A quiet question mark. She handed him the flower.

Gael didn't want it back. It seemed meant for her. But he took it anyway. "Don't worry," he said. "You didn't."

She smiled. "It was nice meeting you," she said again. Cara put her helmet on, lifted a leg over her bike, and pedaled away.

Suddenly, Gael panicked. Was that it? Was he really never going to see her again, this magical girl who had appeared out of nowhere and given him a much-deserved bit of happiness?

"Wait," Gael said.

(I sent a gust of wind at the flower in his hand, but it was no use, he caught it in no time.)

Cara stopped, and Gael hobbled up to her bike, holding out the flower.

"What is it?" Cara asked, balancing one foot on the pavement.

He wasn't quite sure what to do. He hadn't planned this far ahead.

(I wanted so badly to turn him around, to rewind this inopportune encounter, but I couldn't—all I could do was watch it unfold.)

"You should take the flower," Gael said, holding it out to her.

"That's so sweet." Cara took it and wove it into the handlebars. "There. It's lovely." She grabbed the handlebars with both hands. "Well, I'll be going, then."

Gael didn't even know what he was doing. He just knew that he didn't want her to go, didn't want her to bike away and leave him to his emptiness.

And so, with a racing heart and a stomach full of nachos, Gael did the most un-Gael thing of all. He put one hand on her shoulder and another on her cheek, turned her face to his, and planted a kiss right on her lips.

And for a moment, his heart lifted as she returned his kiss.

But then Cara pulled back, and he could see that she was shocked. Gael's face fell for a second. "I'm really sorry. I shouldn't have done that."

"No," she said, backtracking. "I'm just surprised."

"Me, too," he said. "I wasn't planning . . . Well, it just sort of happened. I mean, I don't even know your last name."

Cara seemed to struggle to find her voice. "It's Thompson," she stammered.

"Mine's Brennan. Can I see you again?" he asked. "I would really like that."

Cara stalled. "Again?"

"I mean without having to be hit by your bike. Like, you know, plan something? Run into each other on purpose?"

Cara laughed nervously, and for a second, I thought this whole disaster had been averted.

But then Cara's face changed. "Okay," she said, a cautious smile on her lips. "You're on."

Gael returned her smile, wholly unaware of the girl I had in store for him, the girl who would have been easy to see, if he'd only been looking in the right places. If only I'd worked faster.

I watched, in agony, as his heart lifted just a little.

I was in deep, deep trouble.

And so was he.

how gael became a romantic

AS YOU'VE GLEANED BY NOW, GAEL WAS, QUITE FRANKLY, in love with being in love. And unfortunately for me, his romantic tendencies couldn't simply be undone. They'd been building for quite some time.

Below, a few of the key moments that made him this way.

Age seven:

A rainy recess in second grade. Gael huddled under the metal slide, seeking shelter. A vision of a girl with auburn hair and freckles, drizzle-kissed curls. Mallory Nolastname (she moved to Ohio in third grade; Gael couldn't remember it) took a seat next to him on the dry gravel.

"We're supposed to go inside," she said.

"Okay," said mini-Gael. "Do you want to?" He liked Mallory. She always made a point of sitting at his table during art rotation. She had the 120-pack of crayons, the one with exotic colors like "Desert Sand" and "Macaroni and Cheese," the ones his boring 48-pack didn't have. She let him use whatever colors he wanted, even if he had to fill in almost the whole page, which used a lot.

Mallory stared at him and scooted closer, so their legs were touching, his OshKosh B'gosh jeans and her fuzzy pink tights.

"I love you, Gael."

She kissed him on the cheek.

She ran off.

Then the teacher's aide came out to tell Gael the rest of recess would be held in the classroom, where it wasn't raining.

Even though Mallory Nolastname told two more boys and a girl that she loved them that afternoon, for those brief moments underneath the slide, rain tapping metal like a steel drum serenade, Gael felt more alive than he ever had before.

Age ten:

Valentine's Day. His parents never celebrated it. They'd get him and Piper cards and maybe some of those silly candy hearts, but nothing for each other. His mom said that it was a total Hallmark holiday and that it only existed to empty the pockets of those in relationships. His dad said he didn't like how it made single people feel bad.

Gael was out of toothpaste, and so he went into his parents' room to get some (don't worry, it's not what you're thinking), and there, on the bathroom mirror, scribbled in lipstick:

I love you a little more every year

A secret message, just for his dad. Because no matter how much his mom decried the day, she couldn't help doing something for the person she loved.

Age thirteen:

Eternal. Sunshine. Of. The. Freaking. Spotless. Mind.

Holy hell.

Gael had rented it and watched it with Mason because someone on Reddit said that Charlie Kaufman was pretty much the greatest screenwriter ever. Mason thought it was weird and boring, but Gael watched slack-jawed as a bumbling dude (who vaguely reminded him of himself) and his firecracker of a girlfriend, Clementine, first erased each other from their memories and then struggled to get each other back. The orange-haired Clementine left quite the impression on Gael, his thoughts somewhere along these lines:

If you love someone enough, even if you try and ERASE THEM FROM YOUR MEMORY, they still won't be gone.

Clementine is hot.

Awkward guys can actually get cool girls from time to time.

Love is messy.

I want that.

Age seventeen:

Maybe the most important moment, the one that solidified it all. The one that told him this: that all he'd been waiting for, all he believed in (or *had* believed in, before his parents split), all he'd been searching for since that first declaration under the slide—it was his, and it was there for the taking.

An email from Anika, the day after the planetarium:

> hey–
>
> i thought of you this morning.
>
> it made me happy.
>
> that is all.
>
> xx,
>
> a

missed french connection

GAEL MADE HIS WAY BACK TO HIS HOUSE, THE FRAT hangouts and crappy college apartments turning quickly to tall maples and manicured lawns and cozy porches. As his feet crunched across scattered leaves, he tried to make sense of what had just happened. He had gone from Birthday Dinner Fail to sharing pretty much his favorite meal with an adorable stranger. Whom he'd kissed. On the lips. Out of nowhere. It was almost too much to handle.

Gael knew that he shouldn't get ahead of himself, that he was fresh out of a breakup. There was a reason that they called it a rebound. Because it was clichéd. Obvious.

He kicked at a pile of leaves and tried to push the crazy thought out of his mind.

Clearly, he was a complete mess, he thought, quite reasonably. He didn't need to bring someone else into this.

(I couldn't have agreed more. Which is why I had *planned* to save Gael's real-deal romance for months later, when he was in a better place, at least somewhat. But just like you humans, I don't always get what I want. Far from it.)

Gael was thinking about how soon would be too soon to look Cara up on Facebook, send her a message, when he saw, of all people, Sammy walking down his driveway.

"Oh," she said, startled. She stopped short, right in front of the tree that had been there forever, the one that Mason had fallen out of once, but in his Mason luck, hadn't gotten so much as a scratch. "Hey. I was just leaving. I rode back from the restaurant with your mom."

"Err, sorry for causing a scene," Gael offered.

"It's okay," she said. "It was just a shitty situation."

Apology taken care of, Gael went right back to day-dreaming about Cara. Her cool T-shirt, and her hot sauce thievery, and that way she had of smiling so big . . .

Gael didn't notice the way Sammy tugged at the hem of her dress. He was replaying the kiss in his head, marveling at how something had, almost miraculously, actually gone well for him.

God, was he insane to even think about liking someone so soon? (Yes.)

And if he was insane, did it even matter? (Yes, again.)

Gael felt better than he had since before Anika broke the news via public makeout sesh. His emptiness had turned to lightness, like if he didn't focus on the here and now, he'd float away.

He barely even heard Sammy when she said, "You know, I haven't been completely honest with you . . ."

Sammy stood in front of him with a serious look in her eyes, waiting for him to say the words that would send the truth tumbling out, a truth she'd wanted to divulge for a while but hadn't quite found the right opportunity. (It's easy, Gael. Just listen to the girl. Ask her what she means.)

But (of course) that's not what Gael did.

"Sorry, what?" he asked.

Sammy shook her head quickly. She took two steps back, growing the space between them.

"Nothing," she said. "I'll see you on Monday." She scuttled down the driveway as quickly as her legs could take her, which was very quickly, Sammy being five foot nine, the same height as Gael.

Gael, for his part, headed into his house, not bothering to give Sammy Sutton so much as a second thought.

how to crush a crush
(aka phase one)

DESPITE A FEW CLEVER ATTEMPTS AT TIPPING THE SCALES in my favor (not limited to, but including, both the Internet and phone service temporarily going down at his dad's place), by Sunday, Gael had found Cara on Facebook, and asked her if she wanted to accompany him to REI. He'd decided a nondate was the easiest place to start.

Perhaps he would have been able to wait a bit longer if he hadn't been bored out of his mind at his dad's place that weekend. The apartment was a not-so-cheerful three-bedroom that didn't even have a Blu-ray player. I may have accidentally given Gael's dad HBO access, but not even that could hold Gael off for long—between back-to-back episodes of *Game of Thrones* and Mason's frequent phone calls, none of which he answered, Gael was perpetually reminded that betrayal was *not* reserved to lands filled with dragons and dwarves.

Not to mention his dad was driving him nuts. Gael had apologized to both his mom and dad independently (another fun thing about split households, you had to say everything twice!) and his dad had not only forgiven him, but he seemed intent on finding a way for them to bond. He made attempt after attempt at family fun times (including cooking brunch together, going to the farmers' market, and even indulging in a post-dinner family walk), which only served to make Gael more suspicious that his dad truly did have a reason to feel guilty.

Long story short—Gael *had* to get out of the house. He told Cara he needed something frivolous like wool socks, and he asked if she wanted to offer her expert hiking opinion. She didn't hesitate to say yes.

Ladies and gentleman, it was time to put Phase One of Mission: Directing Gael Away from the Wrong Girl into action. I have a whole treasure trove of proven ways to nip romance in the bud, and with Gael, I was prepared to use any and all within my reach.

Without further ado, behold my handiwork:

First Defense: Annoyance

"Hey!" Cara said eagerly, as she hopped into Gael's car. He'd been idling in front of her dorm for ten minutes past their agreed-upon pick-up time, but she didn't apologize. She buckled her seat belt as Gael pulled away from UNC's South Campus and back toward Highway 54.

"I'm glad you were down to come," Gael said, opting to forgive her lateness. "I remembered you saying you needed hiking boots."

Cara smiled, pulled her long hair into a ponytail, and leaned back in her seat. "Indeed, I do."

She put her feet up on the dash, something Gael always

hated, but he didn't say anything. Instead, he turned up the volume as his new favorite song came on.

After a few seconds, Cara switched to a country station without even asking.

But she *did* ask if they could stop at Starbucks because she *really* wanted a pumpkin spice latte.

(Look, I wasn't using mind control, I promise. *Free will*, yada yada yada. But Cara had censored herself in past relationships, and it was totally fair of me to remind her of that fact. To urge her, ever so slightly, to not hold back, to listen to the music she wanted, embrace her love of Starbucks, literally kick her feet up. Of course, I also happened to know that these very behaviors would annoy Gael to no end.)

Second Defense: Incompatibility

The parking lot in front of REI was for some reason blocked off so Gael and Cara had to park by the movie theater (it's amazing what people will believe when you put up a few official-looking cones). Once out of the car, Gael took in Cara's full outfit. Birkenstocks, ripped jeans, and a Willie Nelson T-shirt. Anika wouldn't have been caught dead looking that laid-back and casual. And yet, he thought, Cara looked great.

"Ready to spend way more money than we should on outdoor gear?" Cara asked eagerly. "And use it for a year and then take advantage of the store's amazing return policy?" She winked and tightened her ponytail. Gael laughed.

As they walked through the parking lot, the autumn sun cast a hard-to-miss glint across the COMING SOON poster. Gael could hardly contain his excitement. "You stoked for the new Wes Anderson movie?"

Cara shrugged.

"What?" he asked. "You think he's overhyped?"

She hopped from the curb to the road and back up again, then grabbed onto the pole of a NO PARKING sign and used her hand to swing around it. In the distance, a fountain trickled happily. "I don't know," Cara said. "To tell you the truth, I don't have much of an opinion. I'm not really that into movies. Except for James Cameron ones. He's pretty much the best director ever."

Third Defense: Jealousy

In REI, Gael and Cara headed past hydration packs and kayaks to the women's shoe area, where Cara grabbed a few pairs of boots to try on. In minutes, a brawny guy who looked like a cross between Mason and Bradley Cooper rushed to help them.

The guy brought out a stack of boxes, and Cara sat down. She slid her feet into the first pair.

"Too tight?" the dude asked as he obnoxiously pinched her toes with his too-big hands.

She shook her head. "Just right," she said with a smirk. Was she flirting with him? Gael wondered.

Cara hopped up, did a couple of paces around the room. She sat back down. "Let me try on the next pair."

The two of them went back and forth like that, and Gael couldn't help but notice that every time Cara walked around, the guy's eyes followed her—and he had a feeling it *wasn't* because he was hoping she'd buy a co-op membership.

Finally, Cara asked to try on the first pair again. After biting her lip and doing yet another lap, she sat down. "I'll take 'em," she said matter-of-factly.

The Not-so-Fortunate Results

Cara turned to Gael and gave him a toothy smile. She wiggled her feet back and forth, and she looked so carefree and enchanting that he found it hard to be turned off by her love of *Titanic* or her penchant for Starbucks specialty drinks.

"Thanks for putting up with me," she said.

"Anytime," Gael said.

But what he thought was—*I'd put up with a lot more to spend time with you.*

Ugh. It was time to step it up with Phase Two.

everyone's an advice columnist these days

THE NEXT DAY, DURING LUNCH AT SCHOOL, GAEL HEADED to his usual spot in the outdoor courtyard. It was already halfway through October, the leaves had fallen, and the temperatures had cooled. No one besides him was still sitting outside, but navigating lunch-table dynamics didn't exactly appeal to Gael.

I won't bore you with the ins and outs of the school cafeteria. Whether from your own experience or from watching movies, you should be familiar with the usual social divisions, and Gael's high school was no exception. Before The Ultimate Betrayal (TUB), Gael had always sat with his own little cohort of not-so-nerdy band nerds—Anika, Jenna, Danny, Mason, and occasionally one or two of the girls from Jenna's AP biology class.

Since TUB, however, Gael had been eating outside alone.

So Gael was quite shocked when, as he sat down on the concrete, leaned against the bricks, and pulled out his Monday usual, a sad ham-and-cheese sandwich his mom had haphazardly thrown together this morning (lunch had been so much better when his dad packed it), he saw Danny and Jenna walking toward him.

"Dude," Danny said, hair neatly combed and gelled, one hand on the strap of his backpack. "Enough of this lunch outside. Come in and sit with us."

Gael took a bite of his sandwich and shook his head.

"Come on," Jenna said. Her own hair was the opposite of Danny's, auburn and wild and frizzy, like she'd just stuck her finger in an electrical socket. They made an odd but cute couple. She looked over to Danny, and he nodded at her. "We miss you," she said. "And it's cold as balls out here."

Danny definitely put her up to that, Gael thought. But still, it was nice.

Gael swallowed and took a sip from his Nalgene bottle. "I have zero desire to sit with Anika and Mason," he said.

"They aren't sitting with us anymore," Jenna said. He detected a hint of annoyance in her voice. She crossed her arms and smiled forcefully.

Danny's smile was more genuine. "We didn't think it was quite fair that they did the wrong thing and you got the shit end of the stick."

Jenna laughed. A few weeks ago at lunch, she'd said "shit end of the stick" accidentally, and it had stuck.

Gael laughed, too. It was pretty funny, no matter how many times you said it.

And he *had* gotten the shit end of the stick. They were right. Why was he letting Mason and Anika's selfishness ruin his other friendships, too?

Without saying anything, Gael grabbed his sandwich and backpack and followed them inside to their usual table. As promised, Anika and Mason were on the opposite end of the cafeteria, eating with two girls from Anika's Bhangra dance group and laughing. He tried to ignore them.

Danny and Jenna spent the next thirty minutes flirtatiously arguing about which season of *Doctor Who* was the best and discussing whether they really needed to do the biology reading or if they should try and Google the answers to the worksheet.

Gael was mostly silent, until Danny, as if a lightbulb had just gone off in his head, stopped talking about bio and looked at him with excitement in his eyes.

"Maybe you need to hook up with somebody else. Especially if she's hotter than Anika."

Jenna smacked him on his ultra-skinny arm. "Could you be any more chauvinistic? He needs some space and to not pull someone else into this drama." She looked at him all serious, and Gael swore even her freckles looked like they weren't messing around. "Like they say on Reddit, lawyer up, delete Facebook, hit the gym. Except for the lawyer part, obviously. Oh, and stop publicly slut-shaming Anika in restaurants."

Eeesh, Gael thought, *brutal*. Was that what he really had done?

He tried to think of a respectful way to defend himself, but Danny shrugged and moved on: "It might be a lot easier to get over Anika if he got under someone else, all I'm saying."

Jenna rolled her eyes. "You just heard that on a bad TV show and wanted a chance to say it."

"Maybe," Danny said, and then he kissed her sloppily.

Between their PDA and conflicting advice, Gael only felt worse. In fact, none of the advice Gael received these days seemed to help:

Last night, his dad had handed him one of the awkward self-help books he had read when he and his mom split up, and then he asked for about the millionth time since the separation if Gael was sure he didn't want to try therapy.

That morning, his mom had begged him to accompany her to a meditation-focused yoga class on Wednesday.

At breakfast, Piper had read him his love horoscope, which suggested he be open to "those who offer deep conversation and intellectual intrigue." (Okay, I was the one who dug up that gem.)

And in chemistry before lunch, Mason had reminded him that now was the time that Gael needed a friend the most. Mason didn't seem to appreciate the irony of the situation.

The problem with the advice he was getting was the problem with almost all advice having to do with me. People suggest what they themselves would want or need. But the act of loving is such a unique experience, it's damn near impossible for anyone but me to know exactly what someone needs at any given time—and even I get it wrong sometimes.

Danny pulled away from Jenna's kiss and fixed his eyes on Gael.

"Come on," he said. "There's got to be some girl you at least think is cute."

Gael certainly wasn't ready to jinx anything by telling them about Cara. One impulsive kiss, plus a trip to REI, did not a relationship make.

So he shook his head and hoped neither Danny nor Jenna could see the color rising to his cheeks.

welcome to the friend zone: temporarily, at least

ON TUESDAY, GAEL ASKED CARA IF SHE WANTED TO TEST out her recent purchase on the Bolin Creek hiking path near his house.

He was surprised by how quickly she said yes.

(Knowing Cara, I wasn't.)

"How are the new shoes?" Gael asked as they stomped along the dirt path, tall trees rising around them.

"Great," Cara said forcefully, though the way she hobbled along made it look like they were anything but.

"Are you sure?" Gael asked. "I can drive us back to your dorm and we could get different shoes. Or we could take a break. Or we could do something totally different if you don't want to hike."

He took a deep breath, reminding himself not to sound so eager. All Gael wanted was an escape from his old life, and this new girl who knew exactly zero of his friends seemed like just the person to give it to him. So long as her feet didn't start bleeding. "Really, we don't have to do this if you don't want," he said.

"I'm fine," she said, as leaves scattered across the path. "They just need to be broken in. Just like the guy at the store said."

Gael forced out visions of that universally good-looking REI dude. Just because Anika put traditional good looks over everything else didn't mean that all girls did.

As the wind whistled through the trees and the creek trilled in the distance and the sunlight made funny shadows on Cara's skin, Gael couldn't help but think about their kiss. It had been wonderful. Unexpected. It had reminded him of his first kiss with Anika. Not in an oh-please-shoot-me-now-I-will-never-forget-about-Anika kind of way. More in a maybe-life-*does*-go-on sort of way.

And she'd kissed back, if only for the tiniest of seconds. He knew that she had.

He forced himself to stop picking the skin on the side of his thumb. REI guy types certainly didn't do that when they were nervous. In fact, the Masons and REI guys of the world didn't ever seem to *get* nervous. *Bastards.*

Gael pointed to a clearing. "If you take that path, it heads to a bench near the creek. We could sit down for a minute and take a break," he said.

"Sweet," Cara said. She skipped up ahead of him, obviously eager to rest her feet.

As he caught up to her, the sound of the rushing creek intensified, matched only by the sound of rushing, pumping blood in his ears. Cara might not be perfect, Gael thought, but who was? So what if she had bad taste in movies and music? So what if she was perpetually late (he'd waited only eight minutes outside her dorm this time)? So what if she wasn't a coffee snob like he was? So what if she was a tad pushy at times . . .

Cara sat down on the rickety bench and immediately loosened the laces on her shoes. Gael noticed a tiny metal plaque he'd never seen before:

FOR MARY, WHO MADE ME HAPPY EVERY DAY.
YOU WILL ALWAYS BE IN MY HEART.

Gael almost wanted to keep walking and find a slightly less sentimental bench, but it was too late. Cara grabbed his hand and pulled him down next to her.

Then again, he thought, maybe the bench was a sign.

(No, Gael. It was *not* a sign.)

Once they were properly seated on the bench of eternal love, Gael opened his backpack and pulled the water bottles out. He handed one to Cara and then drank his down in a few gulps.

"Whoa, there, killer," she said.

Gael laughed nervously. "I guess I was a little thirsty."

He put the cap back on and stuffed the bottle into his backpack. Then he turned to Cara.

Her face was flushed, her forehead shiny, her eyes glistening, her hair pulled into a messy ponytail that never would have passed Anika's standards. Her clothes wouldn't, either: She wore bicycle shorts and a long-sleeve T-shirt from Bandido's, a crappy Mexican restaurant and

Franklin Street institution. The one time he and Anika had gone hiking together, she'd worn hot pink spandex pants, a matching top, and a polka-dot sports bra.

Yet there was something refreshing in the way Cara didn't seem to care about her clothes. Something genuine, honest. Maybe it was illogical, but it didn't seem like a cheater's uniform, that was for sure.

A lock of hair escaped Cara's haphazard updo and danced in the slight breeze from the creek.

The kiss had been great, but the lightness, the escape from numbness, had worn off so quickly. And suddenly all he wanted in the whole wide world was to get it back.

Before he could second-guess himself, Gael reached to tuck the errant lock of hair behind Cara's ear, ran his thumb along her slightly sweaty jawline, and leaned forward, eyes closed . . .

"Wait!"

Gael's eyes snapped open. Cara vigorously shook her head.

For a split second, she looked almost wild with fear, but then she composed herself.

"Gael," she said, her voice soft and slow and drawn out, almost one-note.

Here goes, Gael thought glumly. He stared over her head at the trees, unconsciously picking at his thumb again.

Her words came in a rush, like she was one of those fast-talking, bright-eyed young reporters in a black-and-white movie. "It's not you. You're amazing. It's just that, I know people always say this, but it's *really* not you."

"I wasn't trying to—" Gael hesitated, attempting to craft his words carefully and failing completely. "It's just that I really wanted to kiss you."

Cara blushed, and he swore he saw the tiniest of twinkles in her eye, but she held her hand up. "I know. I mean, I do, too. It's just . . ."

"Just what?" he asked.

Cara took a deep breath and tugged at the waistband of her shorts. She didn't look at him.

"The thing is, I just got out of a relationship a few weeks ago."

"So did I," he offered, neglecting to inform her that "a few weeks" meant two.

She sighed. "Well, the thing is, I told myself I was going to go all of October without dating anyone. And then you kissed me, and, I don't know, I thought maybe it didn't matter, but my suitemates in the dorm, they just thought that it was important that I actually do this, just to prove to myself that I could, you know, be single."

(A classic Serial Monogamist.[3] You may know the type. If not, please see below.)

Gael nodded, but the wheels in his head were already

---

3. Serial Monogamist: One who ruthlessly believes in not being alone. Feelings of love and romance aren't nearly as strong as they are with Romantics; instead, Serial Monogamists have an intense desire to have a partner at every stage of their life. May result in jumping from relationship to relationship, falling for a new person before letting go of the first, and not taking time to figure out who they are on their own. May also result in an uncanny knack for commitment that can help commitment-phobes finally give love a shot.

turning. She liked him enough to tell her roommates about him. She liked him enough to at least think about breaking her promise to herself.

Cara didn't wait for a response. "Is it okay if we just stay friends for now, at least until October is over?"

"Of course it is," he said. And he meant it.

Because there were just over two weeks left in October. He could certainly hold out two weeks.

phase two, explained

OKAY, SO GAEL WASN'T EXACTLY HORRIFIED BY CARA'S less than compatible behavior (leave it to the Manic Pixie Dream Girl trope to convince a guy that someone who straight-up irks him will also somehow save him). *Fine.*

I wasn't worried. I was well into Phase Two.

Cara had made a vow not to date anyone in October. Cara made a lot of vows of that nature. And she always broke them as soon as someone new came into the picture. And her friends always kept their mouths shut.

But through some pivotal moves on my part (an article on how being a good friend means saying what you actually think, a well-timed psychology lecture about how we often lie to those we love most), I'd convinced her friends to speak their minds on this one.

And when *Choosing Me Before We* fell off the shelf at Student Stores, right onto Cara's feet, she took it (rightly) as a sign. She listened.

I'd bought myself a little bit of time—just over two weeks. But I was dealing with a Grade-A Romantic and a textbook Serial Monogamist.

This certainly wasn't going to be easy.

mano a mason

"COME ON, MAN," MASON YELLED FROM HIS TRUCK AS Gael walked home from school on Thursday. "Let me give you a ride!"

Gael always walked to and from school on Thursdays—Gasless Thursdays, one of his dad's earnest efforts to lower their carbon footprint, was a longstanding tradition in the Brennan family, even though they weren't really one family anymore.

Before TUB, of course, Gael had rejoiced in the occasional Thursday-afternoon ride from Anika or Mason, especially if he had his saxophone with him. But now, Mason was the last person he wanted to be around. It had been two days since the hike with Cara, and he wavered between counting down the days to November and wondering if her whole story was just a lame excuse to reject him.

He and Cara had made plans to go to a UNC exhibition basketball game together, but it wasn't until Friday, which left him no choice but to slog through his classes, make inane lunchtime chitchat with Danny and Jenna, and listen to his mother's daily reminders about how being single could be empowering, freeing—the perfect time to find yourself!—which was completely hard to believe given how puffy her eyes had been these last few months. Honestly, Gael was exhausted.

Both mentally *and* physically.

Because that morning he'd made the deranged decision to go running with his dad. After ten blocks, Gael had gotten winded, and after another ten, his dad finally realized that chanting "You can do it!" was about as helpful as telling a sloth to hurry up. A few blocks later Gael screamed, "This was the shittiest idea ever!" and he headed back home before he could see the inevitable disappointment on his dad's face.

Mason, ex–best friend and king of the betrayers, laid on the horn.

"What the hell, man?" Gael finally broke his silence, accompanying his question with a choice gesture.

Gael picked up his pace, but Mason matched it—driving his truck well below the speed limit.

"Seriously?" Gael asked, turning around.

"We need to talk," Mason said. "Manna to manna."

A line of cars steadily backed up behind Mason. Horns honked, but Mason wouldn't go any faster.

"Fine," Gael snapped. He walked around the truck, opened the passenger door, and tossed his backpack in harder than he needed to.

"And, by the way, it's *mano a mano*," Gael said bitterly, as he slammed the door and Mason stepped on the gas. "Manna is, like, ancient bread."

Mason shrugged, and then despite his decree, he didn't say anything the entire drive to Gael's house, which was thankfully only about five minutes.

As soon as Mason pulled into his driveway, Gael got out of the car and slammed the door without so much as a word of thanks. In classic Mason fashion, he didn't take the hint. Instead, he turned the car off, got out, and followed Gael inside.

Sammy was sitting in her usual spot in the dining room with Piper. Upon seeing Mason, she adjusted her glasses, waiting to be clued in on any new developments in the Gael-Mason drama she'd so epically witnessed at his birthday dinner. Gael passed by without so much as a "Hi" and headed to his room. Mason followed.

Mason flipped on Gael's Xbox and loaded up his file in Skyrim like nothing was the matter. He shot Gael a goofy grin as a rugged landscape appeared on the screen. This used to be their thing. Skyrim was Gael's favorite video game (it reminded him of *Lord of the Rings*), and they'd spent hours taking turns upgrading their armor, slaying dragons, and defending themselves against thieving bandits.

Gael felt a brief—but deep—pang in his chest. He missed Mason. It was kind of like they'd broken up, too. But as soon as the feeling came, he pushed it away. Mason was trying so hard to act like things were okay. But they weren't. And Gael didn't really think they ever would be again. What Mason had done was completely inexcusable.

It went against every rule of friendship. Every rule of basic human decency.

Gael laughed bitterly to himself: kind of like barging into someone's home to play video games without being invited.

Mason's Skyrim character ran through the woods, his attractive female servant trailing behind him. He shot an arrow at a wanderer, killing him instantly.

"You know you shouldn't do that," Gael said.

Mason shrugged. "Gotta get in my archery practice. Some must die in the pursuit of greatness."

Gael sat down on the bed. "You can't just go around killing people who did nothing to you."

Mason gave him a side glance. "That never bothered you before."

"Well, it does now." Gael's voice was loud, agitated. "That guy could have helped you. You, *literally*, just stabbed him in the back."

He turned to Gael, and for a second, it looked like he was maybe actually going to say something more than his vague, "I'm sorry, dude," but he didn't.

Instead, Mason killed two wolves and a bandit before he spoke again. "The thing is, I need your help."

Gael scoffed. "I am in no mood to help you."

"Just hear me out." Mason's character headed into a cave, using a spell to light the way. "Things have been weird with Anika."

Gael grabbed a pillow and punched it down. "Are you

kidding me? You hijacked my afternoon and invaded my space to get advice about the girlfriend *you stole from me?*"

(Mason's actions *were* kind of ridiculous. But what Gael still couldn't wrap his head around was that *everyone* makes ridiculous choices when it comes to me. This wasn't *The Gael Show*. He wasn't the only one who had ever been in love.)

Mason paused the game, grabbed Gael's computer chair, whipped it around, and sat down backward. He leaned his chest against the back of the chair and let his extra-long arms dangle at the sides. "She's not a possession, dude," Mason said, in a totally profound and un-Mason way. It almost made Gael feel like a jerk. "She's a person."

"Whatever," Gael said. "However you want to say it, it was a pretty shitty thing to do."

Mason picked at a sticker on the back of the chair. "I know. And maybe the longer you go without talking to me, the more I get just how shitty it was. But you're the only one I feel comfortable talking about stuff like this with . . ."

Gael crossed his arms and kept his mouth shut.

Mason took a deep breath and swiveled the chair back and forth. "Just so you know, *she* kissed *me*, okay?"

Gael threw his hands up in the air. "I already told you, I do not want to hear about how you and Anika got together."

Mason stared at his feet, then back up at Gael.

"Look, I should have told her to break up with you before even thinking about doing anything with me, but I didn't, okay? And now . . . I don't know, I guess I'm worried that she's messing with both of us. Like what if she doesn't care about me at all and was just using me to break up with you?"

Gael rolled his eyes. "Well, would you even care? Isn't that the Mason goal? No one to tie you down?"

Mason crossed his arms and leaned forward in the chair. "The thing is, sometimes she doesn't wear a freaking seat belt when she's in my truck, and then I think about what if there are other times that she's not wearing a seat belt, and what if there's some sort of accident, and then what if she's just gone, and . . . well . . ."

"What do seat belts have to do with this?" Gael asked.

Mason shrugged and mumbled, "I never worried about little things like that before. Half the time, I don't even wear a seat belt."

"That's because you're an idiot," Gael said.

But behind his rebuke, there was the weirdest thing—happiness for his friend. Mason actually cared, legitimately cared, about a girl. Not just because she was hot or because he wanted to hook up with her, but just because she was her. Mason, who Gael had often feared would grow up to be a total womanizer, sacrificing any chance of real happiness in the name of perky boobs, had somehow stumbled upon the real deal.

For a fraction of a second, Gael was proud of his friend.

(And I was, too. Mason was a natural Drifter,[4] but for once in his life, he had no inclination to run.)

Gael pushed his sympathy away. How Mason had gotten to this point was still utterly unforgiveable. "So what exactly do you want me to do?" he asked.

"Is this normal?" Mason asked. "To worry like this?"

(Boys. Yes, it's normal! Your mother was telling the truth when she said she worries because she loves you.)

Gael's patience had run its course. "I have *no idea* what normal is for people like you," he said with disdain. "Now can you get the hell out of my room, please?"

Mason paused for an agonizing moment, but then he reluctantly grabbed his bag and headed out. Gael waited until the door was shut behind him before he unpaused Skyrim, wandered through the woods, and shot the first stranger he could find in the back.

It didn't feel as good as he'd imagined it would.

---

4. Drifter: One who primarily seeks solitude and freedom from "being tied down" in romantic trysts. May result in missed opportunities, "ghosting," general douchebaggery, and perpetual bachelor- or bachelorette-hood. May also result in a high level of self-awareness and confidence in relationships they don't immediately flee.

throwback to the first
"i love you": mason edition

ALL RIGHT, ALL RIGHT, GAEL AND MASON HAD NEVER actually said "I love you" to each other (unless, of course, you count that one time Mason had a few too many beers, and Gael had to hold his shaggy hair back), but even without the official words, their love had been sealed since they were about eleven years old.

That was the year that Gael, cursed with oily skin from his stupid dad, got his first real breakout. And we're not talking a clogged pore or two like the models on the Clearasil commercials. We're talking legit, mountainous, impossible-not-to-look-at zits. So big you couldn't even call them pimples.

It didn't take long for the über-creative minds of Gael's middle school to think of a few names to use instead of "Gael"—think "pizza face," "crater face," and the only one that was actually a little clever, yet still completely cruel, "Orion."

It all came to a head (sorry) the day Brad Litcherson turned to Gael in first-period language arts and said, "Dude, are you wearing makeup?"

Gael's face turned beet red (at least the parts that weren't covered up by the concealer he'd borrowed from his mom). Gael stormed out of the room before he could even hear Mason tell Brad to "shut the eff up" or their teacher, Mrs. Jackson, try to calm them all down.

The next morning, Gael walked into language arts feeling especially vulnerable, with a face free of concealer and his zits on display for all to see. But all the kids were crowded around Mason's desk.

Gael pushed through them to grab his seat.

Mason was sitting back in his chair—like it was no big deal—in full makeup. Foundation. Concealer. Powder. Blush. Eyeliner. Bright blue eye shadow with sparkles. Mascara. (Mason had an older sister who'd helped him go to town.)

Kids were laughing, taking pictures on their phones. No one even looked at Gael. Barely anyone even remembered that Gael had been caught wearing concealer only the day before. Brad freaking Litcherson sat slouched in his desk, defeated.

Mrs. Jackson told everyone to sit down and ignore "Mason's obvious ploy for attention" (she later got scolded by administrators for pushing traditional gender identities on her students), but Gael could only whisper to Mason, "You're such a weirdo."

"And you're best friends with a weirdo," Mason said.

"Thanks, man," Gael said.

"Anytime." Mason batted his eyelashes at him.

The kids called Mason "Cover Girl" for the rest of the year.

And no one said anything about Gael's acne after that.

# of all the bedrooms
in all the towns in all the world
she had to walk into mine

THE TEXT FROM MASON CAME ALMOST IMMEDIATELY after he'd left Gael's:

p.s. sammy got hotter since i last saw her, u should ask her out

Not a moment later, Sammy opened Gael's door.

Embarrassed, Gael shoved his phone deep under the covers and went back to focusing on the game, where his character stood over the man he'd just killed.

Sammy walked in the room without asking if it was okay and put a hand on her hip, her neutral position. "So what was that about?"

For a second, Gael thought she was talking about the text. It was *so like Mason* to come over, practically profess his love for Anika, and then drool over another girl on the way out the door.

"You and Mason are friends again?" she asked, relaxing and dropping her hand to the side.

It's not like Sammy and Mason really knew each other, but until recently, Mason had been over so frequently that they at least knew each other's status. Sammy: resident babysitter. Mason: best friend. Recently updated to *former* best friend.

"No," Gael stumbled. "He just barged in."

She tilted her head ever so slightly to the side, her short hair framing her face in a perfect black arc. She looked kind of like Uma Thurman's character in *Pulp Fiction*, bangs and all. She wore a tight *Casablanca* T-shirt that Gael couldn't help but appreciate, skinny jeans, and a long geometric necklace that drew your eye to all the right places. Gael looked away.

Sure, she was good-looking, Gael thought. Mason was right. But she was so obviously *trying* to be cool. Besides, a *Casablanca* T-shirt looked cool no matter who wore it.

"This is the guy who stole your girlfriend, right?" Sammy asked.

He didn't answer, and she turned her gaze to the TV. "Getting out your aggression through video games?" She rolled her eyes. "Nice."

Gael put down the controller. "Don't tell me, you're anti–video games? How *original*."

"So it's cliché to dislike things that are proviolence and antiwomen?" she retorted. "Umm, hello, gamer gate."

Gael had gotten the video-game lecture ad nauseum from his mother. He didn't need to hear it again. "I know, I know," he said. "But this one has morals. I killed that guy, but I'm going to pay for it later. I probably shouldn't have done that."

Sammy raised her eyebrows at him and tilted her head to the side. "Really?"

"Really," he said.

"So you'll, like, go to jail?"

Gael shook his head. "Probably not. But I'll pay for it. Don't worry."

She uncrossed her arms, let them hang at her sides, gave him a small smile. "So are you going to tell me about your ex-friend barging in, or are you going to debate me on the value of violent video games? If it's the latter, please know that I will most definitely school you."

Gael hesitated. He and Sammy's conversations had always been fairly surface level. The thought of pouring out his relationship drama to someone in a stable long-term thing—someone who hadn't been dumped publicly and who hadn't entered into a pseudo-relationship with someone with such big issues around not being alone that she had to make *rules* about not dating for a month—well, it felt a little pathetic.

Then again, it would be nice to be able to talk to *someone*. Especially someone who wasn't the cause of the whole thing.

He flipped off the TV. "I'm kind of all over the place this week."

"Umm, shouldn't you be?" she asked, turning her body to him in a way that made him feel, suddenly, like he could say anything. "Because having an ex show up at my birthday dinner would definitely send me into a tailspin of anxiety."

Gael laughed. "If that wasn't enough, Mason just

followed me home to tell me he's in love with Anika and ask my advice."

Sammy gasped. "He said he was in *love?*"

Gael shook his head. "No, but he might as well have. He obviously cares about her."

"And you still love her?" Sammy asked, settling down to sit on the floor, back against his wall.

(I could see what Gael couldn't, that Sammy was hoping he'd say no. She told herself that it was because Anika was a narcissist, and Gael deserved better. But I had an inkling that wasn't the whole story. And my inklings are pretty spot-on.)

"Actually, more and more, I don't think I do." Gael took a deep breath. "I guess it was easier to just think of them cheating as this super-shitty thing, and if they really care about each other, it feels less shitty. I don't know."

Sammy narrowed her eyes at him. "What's going on here?" she asked. "There is no way that Gael Brennan would just be all Dr. Phil about this. What are you not telling me?"

Gael blushed. "I think I might like someone else," he said.

Sammy paused. "Really?" she asked cautiously. "So soon after Anika?"

Gael stared down at his hands, then back to Sammy. He was embarrassed—he knew he sounded foolish—but he'd already told her this much, he might as well tell her the whole thing. "I randomly met her walking home from my birthday dinner, and then out of the blue I just kissed her—it was crazy—and we've hung out twice since then, but on Tuesday she told me that basically she's fresh out of a relationship and doesn't want to date anyone this month."

Sammy laughed. Or, he wondered, was it more of a scoff? "Wow, a *whole month* without dating someone. What a sacrifice!"

Gael scooted back on the bed and crossed his arms. "Real easy to judge. It's not like you've had loads of time to deal with being single."

There was a brief pause, but Sammy just pressed her lips together and stood up. "I'm just saying, maybe two people who are obviously hung up on other people shouldn't just jump into something because they ran into each other in the street."

Her words were bold and strong, like bitter, burnt coffee. "But what if there's a *reason* why we met," he asked, a little vehemently. As he racked his brain for a way to support his case, his eyes landed, once again, on her shirt. Bingo. He nodded to it. "Like in *Casablanca*. Ilsa and Victor running into each other again."

Sammy laughed, then shook her head. "And if you remember the ending, it didn't work out."

"That's only because it was in war-torn Morocco," Gael said, his voice gaining strength. He may have been badly and obviously rebounding, but he could at least make his point with movies. "Anywhere else and it would have."

Sammy rolled her eyes. "Life isn't a rom-com. Much as I love them, they aren't real."

Gael momentarily forgot his point. "*You* love rom-coms?"

"I do," she said, her shoulders relaxing a bit. "Do you have a problem with that?"

Gael laughed. "No, I just expected someone who was obsessed with French lit to have a bit more sophisticated movie taste."

"Hey," Sammy said. "I'm not *that* big of a snob."

Gael found that debatable, but he let it go.

Sammy shrugged. "I'm just saying, timing is important. And maybe two people who both have really recent baggage shouldn't rush in."

(She was right, of course. Hence the need for my job.)

"So you're telling me you *didn't* rush when you met John?" Gael asked indignantly.

"What are you guys talking about?"

Gael and Sammy whipped around to see Piper standing in the doorway.

Sammy discreetly wiped her hand under her eyes and then cocked one hip to the side. "*Casablanca*," she said. "And the girl Gael currently has a crush on."

"You have a crush on someone!" Piper squealed.

"None of your business," Gael said, blushing again and feeling thoroughly outnumbered. "And even if I did, Sammy thinks it's a bad idea."

Piper's eyes volleyed from Sammy to Gael and back again. Then she smiled her wonderful-world-of-Wikipedia smile, the smile of having learned a new, useful fact.

"Well, all I know is, if Sammy doesn't think you should

be with her, she must have a good reason. Come on, Sammy," Piper said. "We still have four translations left!"

Piper stomped out of the room, dragging Sammy by the hand.

"You're the boss!" Sammy said to Piper, leaving Gael alone with his thoughts.

gael's evening search queries, in chronological order

5:03 P.M. how can you tell if you're rebounding

5:06 P.M. am I rebounding quiz

5:15 P.M. serial monogamist definition

5:17 P.M. dating a new person after being cheated on

5:28 P.M. what does it mean when a girl says can we just be friends for now

5:40 P.M. famous quotes from casablanca about love

6:05 P.M. dating a college girl while in high school

6:12 P.M. the girl i like doesn't like movies

6:29 P.M. girl says she likes me but doesn't want to date for two weeks is she blowing me off

6:40 P.M. is going to a basketball game a date

6:43 P.M. what if I'm alone forever

a house divided

THE NEXT EVENING, AS GAEL PREPARED TO LEAVE THE house for his Friday-night pseudo-date with Cara, his mom stopped him in the front hallway.

"Where are you going?" she asked.

Gael reached for the doorknob with one hand and tugged at the logo on his sweatshirt with the other. "There's a basketball game tonight. I have tickets."

His mom sighed loudly and crossed her arms against her tiny frame. Then she grabbed a trinket from the foyer table, dusted it with the bottom of her shirt, and put it back. "When were you going to tell me? You're supposed to have dinner with your dad tonight."

Gael shrugged. "I already told Dad. He said he has extended office hours tonight anyway, and he'd pick up Piper for dinner after he was done."

"Well, you didn't tell me," his mom snapped.

Gael let go of the doorknob and crossed his arms. "I'm telling you now. Plus, the fact that you and Dad suck at communicating with each other really isn't *my* problem."

For a second, his mom looked shocked at his frankness, but then she shook her head. "You know, you're really supposed to be hanging out with your dad on Friday nights. You owe it to him."

Gael sighed. "So I'm not allowed to do anything on Fridays just because you guys split up?" he asked. "How is that fair?"

That's when Piper breezed in, an electric-green tutu around her waist and a toy lightsaber in her hand. She pouted. "You never used to bail out when we had family movie night."

She was right. Family movie night had been a semi-religious experience in the Brennan household. Every Friday, they ordered Papa John's and took turns picking out a movie to watch as a family. Piper usually made them watch either a nature documentary or some tweeny friendship story; his dad gravitated toward modern psychological dramas and underdog boxing flicks; his mom almost always picked something black-and-white and unapologetically optimistic; and Gael felt it was his moral duty as the resident film snob to mix it up. As much as he could while keeping things Piper-appropriate, that is.

Gael scoffed. "Well, it's not *my* fault family movie night is over. *I'm* not the one who decided to get divorced."

His mom's jaw dropped, and Piper's chin began to shake. "They're not divorced," his little sister said. "They're just living separately." She looked like she might cry.

"I'm sorry," Gael said, looking from Piper to his mom. "But I don't know what to say."

His mom knelt down to hug Piper. "Just go," she said. "I'll take her over to Dad's."

Gael nodded and headed out the door, though the prospect of seeing Cara no longer made him feel better. His family was broken. It was the honest, simple truth.

No girl was going to fix that.

after-office hours

AS PER USUAL, CARA WAS NOT OUTSIDE HER DORM AT their agreed-upon meeting time, so Gael pulled in front of the building and let the car idle.

His eyes drifted out the window toward the students on campus.

To the couple walking hand in hand into a nearby dorm.

To the emo-looking kid bumming a cigarette from a guy in a preppy polo.

To the girl in neon-orange track pants running faster than he ever would in his life.

To his dad, following an attractive girl toward Carmichael Hall . . .

Gael whipped his head back and squinted his eyes. It was his dad, for sure, with his annoying fall knit hat and his corduroy professor jacket and a stupid smile on his face.

And the girl next to him hardly looked like she could be older than twenty-three. A grad student, maybe, but possibly even an undergrad.

Gael's heart started to race. When the secret phone calls started, he'd toyed with the idea that his dad was cheating, but until now, he'd never really truly believed it.

But why else would he have lied about having office hours? Why in the world would he be going into one of the dorms? They were a good ten-minute walk from his dad's office. There was no logical reason to be here.

Unless . . .

"Jesus *Christ!*"

A sudden knock on the car window made Gael jump. Cara was there, staring at him.

He unlocked the door robotically.

"Everything okay?" she asked as she got in the car. "I didn't mean to scare you."

Gael nodded, and then looked quickly back toward Carmichael, both afraid to see anything more and afraid of not seeing anything more.

His dad and the girl were gone.

"Are you sure?" Cara asked.

His face suddenly felt hot, and he thought he might cry, but he forced himself to smile. He forced himself not to focus on what he had just seen. He couldn't fall apart. Not in front of the one person who hadn't already seen him at his worst.

"Just a little tired is all," he stammered. He shifted into drive and pulled forward before she could ask anything else.

friend-zone defense

BY THE TIME THEY WERE INSIDE THE DEAN DOME, IN THEIR tiny squished seats, Gael's primary concern was making sure Cara didn't see that his eyes were still glassy—that he was on the verge of completely falling apart.

He couldn't get the vision of his dad walking toward the dorm out of his mind, no matter how much he tried to distract himself with the fast-paced game in front of him.

The tallest guy on their team sunk a three-pointer, and the crowd roared, UNC's ram mascot springing into cartwheels while a cheerleader did a back flip. Cara's rally cry was loud, high-pitched, and long. Her enthusiasm should have been endearing, but Gael only found it grating. Cara jumped out of her seat, but he couldn't bring himself to follow.

The opposing team grabbed the ball and was on the other end of the court in seconds.

"You okay?" Cara asked, sitting back down.

"Yeah," Gael lied. Then he whipped his head away immediately and attempted to discreetly wipe the moisture from his eyes.

Cara either didn't notice or decided to give him space

because her gaze stayed focused on the players below. Gael was grateful for that, at least.

There was a round of squeaks against the glossy hardwood floor, and the point guard pivoted, evading the guy blocking him, and made a two-point shot for Carolina.

Gael eyed the 2009 National Championship flag that hung from the rafters of the Dean Dome. His family had had season tickets that year. Piper was practically a newborn, but they'd still managed to make it to almost every game, Gael in his little-kid jersey, shaking noisemakers like it was his job. They'd even been in the Dean Dome to watch the championship game on the Jumbotron as Carolina squashed Michigan State far away in chilly Detroit. They'd followed the crowd of students to Franklin Street, and Gael got to watch a few college kids jumping around and setting things on fire before his mom had said they really should go. The next day, his dad had pointed out that even the president of the United States was a Carolina fan. They'd gotten five copies of the *Daily Tar Heel* and framed one in their basement.

None of that would happen for Piper, he thought, because his family wasn't his family anymore.

Because his dad had turned his family into something awful.

Suddenly, Gael was no longer on the brink of tears. Instead, he seethed with anger.

"Don't you find it completely ridiculous that they have 'Carolina' printed on their butts?" Cara asked, breaking his train of thought.

Gael took a deep breath and tried to focus on acting like a normal human being.

"I don't exactly make a point of staring at other guys' butts," he said, forcing a laugh.

Cara laughed loudly and leaned back farther in her chair. She kicked her feet up, placing her exposed toes dangerously close to the head of the guy in front of them. "You know it doesn't make you gay just for having eyes," she said.

Gael sighed as Cara removed her feet from the chair and went back to a normal sitting position. "All right, all right. I have noticed, and it is kind of ridiculous, yes."

Cara wiggled her eyebrows up and down. "Look at you, checking out other guys' butts!"

She laughed.

And so did Gael, his anger dissipating the tiniest bit.

(I was torn, to be honest. On the one hand, I ached to give Gael some relief from what he'd seen. But on the other, I worried that tonight would only push him even harder toward Cara, toward escape. She wasn't right for him, and no matter what was going on in his life, I had to help him understand that.)

"Thanks," Gael said. The halftime clock buzzed and the crowd burst into cheers. UNC was up by twenty-two.

"For what?" Cara asked.

He shrugged. "For the tickets. For running into me on your bike when I needed a friend."

Cara gazed at him a touch too long, but then a guy

cleared his throat, and she and Gael looked up. The guy was waiting to get past, and she tucked her feet underneath her seat, letting him by.

(Just a little thing, but it was important to break that moment, trust me.)

When the guy was gone, she looked back down at the court, fiddled with her ponytail, wiggled her toes in her Birks. "Should we get some food?"

Gael nodded. "I can get some if you watch my stuff." He wasn't sure if he could stomach food right now, but he could at least try. "I always go for the pulled pork sandwiches here. You want one?"

"Sounds perfect," she said. "You da best."

I watched with a bittersweet ache as Gael broke into his first real smile of the night.

a peek into gael's future

YOU THINK I'M CRUEL, DON'T YOU? I KNOW YOU DO.

You're thinking that Gael has just seen something that would send anyone into crisis mode, and so what if the girl who is helping him through it is not the perfect girl for him?

You're wondering whether rebounding really is the worst thing on earth, especially during a time of his life so fraught with pain and heartbreak. He's a kid, after all. So what if this isn't the real deal? He'll have plenty of chances after this.

And you're right . . . partially, at least. Lots of people go after the wrong person. Lots of people get second or third or fourth or fifteenth chances at the real deal.

But it wasn't as simple as Gael just moving on to the next one, either.

Remember back at the beginning when I told you about the Rules? When I said, and I quote, "Real love makes you better than you ever knew you could be." I wasn't just blowing smoke. Here's the thing—those words could not possibly apply more appropriately to Gael. Because I could peek into the future, and this is what I saw:

I saw Gael's love of movies working so beautifully with his love of, well, *love*.

I saw him, years down the road, drawing on his own experience of young, authentic love to make a gorgeous, heartbreaking movie that rocked the festival circuit and put him on the map as a promising new director.

I saw a girl who would encourage him, always, to be his best self, to go after everything that he wanted. Whose own passion inspired him day after day.

I saw a career of him making these sorts of movies, ones that inspired people to believe in love the world over.

Some people might even call them romantic comedies, though he'd always protest the association with his least favorite genre.

I *may* have even seen a shiny statue in his future.

I'm not saying that the romance I had in store for eighteen-year-old Gael would last forever. But I am saying that, no matter how long it lasted, this one would change his life—and the lives of others—for many years to come.

And on the other hand? If my machinations didn't come to fruition?

Well, I saw that future, too. I saw the ache of another bitter heartbreak when Cara eventually got tired of the newness of it all.

I saw a desk job. Maybe a movie review blog on the side. Some good dates here and some bad dates there, and maybe, when he was old enough, he'd marry a nice girl and settle down.

He'd keep up with the Joneses and polish his car on the weekends and tell himself that he would go to more movies if only he had the time.

It wasn't necessarily a bad life.

But it wasn't what Gael's life was supposed to be.

And I was the only one who could fix it.

friend-zone defense, continued

THE SECOND HALF OF THE GAME STARTED, AND WITH the greasy sandwich in front of him, Gael found his appetite. He and Cara devoured their sandwiches, while UNC maintained their lead. When he was finished, he licked the barbecue sauce off his fingers instead of using a napkin, something Anika had always despised. Feeling slightly less distraught, he joined Cara in yelling at the refs, another thing Anika hated. Sure, until about five minutes ago, Gael had kind of hated it, too. But this was the new Gael. The uninhibited Gael. The Gael who realized that no one else was playing by the rules, his father included, and he didn't need to, either. Cara may not be perfect, she may not do everything exactly as he did, but at least she was here.

(Gael was so far gone by this point that he didn't even realize how sad that type of logic is.)

As the mammoth players sunk basket after basket, Gael stopped thinking about his dad and his family. He felt good. He felt alive. He felt like the world could go on, even though it wasn't going the way he'd planned.

And that's when he looked at Cara and saw she was

looking at him, her eyes inviting, her face flushed from yelling, strands of hair that had escaped her ponytail delicately framing her face. And that's when he thought to himself, screw November. Why in the world does it matter if we wait for November?

And that's when he guessed she was thinking the same thing.

(And that's when I saw my moment.)

The horn blew, signaling a time-out, and Gael and Cara were shocked out of their secret little world, just as Cara's ex-boyfriend, Branson, came walking up the steps in search of his own pulled pork sandwich.

Their eyes locked, and I could almost feel the instant ache in Cara's belly, the hurt that washed over her, head to toe.

I knew it could have gone a few ways, as these things always do. She could have smiled and waved and struck up a conversation with him and tried to act like everything was normal while practically ignoring Gael and downplaying their whatever-it-was.

Or she could have looked down at her feet, waited until Branson walked by, head filled with the thoughts of how much she still cared about him, of how clearly she did not care about Gael.

Or she could have done what she did. The one thing I'd been hoping and praying for her *not* to do.

The band burst into a rendition of "Carolina on My Mind" and Cara jumped to her feet, grabbing Gael's hand

and pulling him up with her, snaking her arm around his back in time for Branson to see.

I'd underestimated Cara's bitterness, her desire to make Branson jealous, no matter what the cost to Gael.

Cara wasn't a bad person—please don't judge her—it's just that people do crazy things when it comes to me.

Of course, Gael didn't see any of that. To Gael, the girl he liked had her arm around him and was swaying back and forth as his favorite song filled the stadium.

To Gael, a place that was filled with painful family memories would now have a new memory—a memory of her.

"You're the best for getting these tickets," he said. And he meant it. With all his heart.

when cara met sammy

THE NEXT MORNING, I ABANDONED MY POST MONITORING Gael and his ever-vacillating emotions to launch a special mission, part of what I was calling Operation Get Gael's Love Life Back on Track.

Just after 9:00 A.M., I headed to the campus dining hall where I knew Sammy Sutton would be.

What most people didn't know about Sammy was that she was obsessed with chocolate. She even found Gael's Snickers habit endearing, as much as she made fun of him for it. It was the kind of thing she would do. Scratch that, it was the kind of thing she *did* do. Her chocolate-chip waffle habit actually began on September 4, to be exact, the day John dumped her, during the second week of school. (Fun fact: The first two weeks of college are breakup city, no matter where in the world you are.)

However, because her mom used to tell her that the stuff would make her fat, she sadly associated chocolate with shame and therefore hid her love well. But on Saturday mornings, just a few minutes after the dining hall opened, while her hallmates were still sleeping off their hangovers, she religiously made herself a big Belgian waffle loaded with chocolate chips, enjoying her guilty pleasure all on her own.

Cara was also a waffle-lover. But she normally got to the dining hall a good bit later. Of course, normally, her alarm didn't mysteriously go off at eight forty-five on a Saturday. And so when she would usually be sleeping, she was lying in her bed, cursing herself for somehow not turning off her weekday alarm, and trying to go back to sleep.

By 9:15 Cara was begrudgingly throwing on her Birks and heading to the dining hall in attempt to get on with her day, since she clearly wasn't going to nod off again.

The two strangers got to the waffle station at exactly the same time. (I swear I'm like an award-winning orchestra conductor sometimes.)

Cara poured a ladleful of regular batter onto her machine, while Sammy poured her own ladle and grabbed the container of chocolate chips.

Wait for it . . .

Wait for it . . .

"Shit!" Sammy stared at the mountain of chocolate now piled up on the batter. The cap of the container had come off completely and rolled along the floor right into Cara's feet.

"Oh my god, let me help you!" Cara sprung to action, as I knew she would, grabbing a broom and dustpan that I'd placed nearby and cleaning up the chips on the floor.

"Oh, you don't have to," Sammy stammered. "I'm sorry—I don't know how that happened."

Cara swept the chips into the dustpan and surveyed

Sammy's half-cooked waffle, which was now completely coated in messy, gooey chocolate. "I mean, I love chocolate as much as the next girl, but even that's a little much for me."

Sammy laughed, then fiddled with the container in her hand. "I think some dick unscrewed the top so they'd all fall out." She rolled her eyes. "College boys." (Or metaphysical entities. Either one.)

"Wow, what an asshole," Cara said. "People are such idiots."

The girls carefully threw their ruined waffles into the trash, then Cara poured new waffles for both of them and topped Sammy's with an appropriate amount of chips. She closed the lids, and the smell of melting chocolate filled the air. "I'm Cara, by the way," she said.

"Sammy." She reached out her hand. "And thank you so much for your help."

"No problem. Are you here with anyone?" Cara asked. "I feel like after surviving a chocolate debacle the least we could do is eat our waffles together. I woke up super early today, so none of my friends are here."

Sammy smiled. "You're on."

They grabbed seats at a two-person table and proceeded to chat about everything from waffles to the tininess of their dorm rooms to the idiocy of the teacher's assistant in Sammy's French philosophy class. The two bonded brilliantly, as I knew they would.

As Sammy cut apart the last bit of her waffle, she got an idea. (Yes, there *may* have been some nudging from yours truly.)

"This is kind of random," she said. "But I actually have a Groupon for two tickets to the zoo in Asheboro tomorrow, and my roommate bailed. Any chance you want to go?"

Cara laughed out loud. "That is random."

Sammy topped off her last bite with extra syrup. "I know, but animals are fun, right?"

Cara smiled. "Totally. You're on."

And just like that my plan was back on track.

meanwhile, on the other side of town

"HOW DOES YOUR APARTMENT HAVE, LIKE, NO SERVICE?" Gael asked as he stormed out of the sad bedroom in his dad's apartment and slammed the door behind him.

In the tiny apartment kitchen, Gael's dad stirred eggs and fried bacon while Piper cut the tops off strawberries. They were wearing matching aprons that Gael's mom had gotten the whole family a couple of Christmases ago. Piper's said "Good Egg" and his dad's said "Bad Egg."

"It works fine in the living room," his dad said, as he turned over a piece of bacon with tongs.

"I would like at least a little privacy," Gael said bitterly.

"It works fine in my room, too," his dad offered.

The thought of making his phone call where his dad ostensibly spent time talking to that girl made Gael sick to his stomach. "I want to talk in *my own room*," he said angrily.

Piper stopped cutting fruit long enough to cross her arms and purse her lips. "Maybe you shouldn't be, like, addicted to your phone? Mom says you spend way too much time with your gadgets."

"Well, Mom's not here, is she?" Gael snapped.

His dad put his tongs down and stared at him. "You don't have to say it like that. We're all trying the best we can."

Gael just rolled his eyes. "The bacon's burning," he said, as the smell of smoke filled the air. He headed to the couch while his dad flipped on the fan and Piper ran around the kitchen, whipping a towel around in an attempt to diffuse the smoke.

Ever since Gael was old enough to look after Piper, their family's Saturday morning tradition had been for his dad to go for a long run, while his mom went to yoga class. Around 11:00 they'd gather back at home for brunch.

Which had all been good and fine before they split. Now his dad's attempts to make it just like it always was just felt pathetic, and like he was obviously trying to make up for something. Even the smell of bacon, previously Gael's favorite food, had come to bother him.

Gael sat down and tapped at Cara's contact on his phone. As the phone rang, he stared at the chipped paint on the wall near the ceiling. The all-white walls of this place were nothing like his house, with colors his mom had picked out and warm polished wood furniture and their fancy chemical-free laundry detergent smelling simultaneously of lavender and home.

In comparison, his dad's apartment was bright and dingy, and the balcony that shot out from the living room was a sad excuse for a yard. Not to mention said balcony didn't have cell service, either.

"Hello," Cara answered, as the apartment's smoke detector went off.

"Hey," Gael said. "Sorry. Can you make that stop?" he yelled at his dad.

"Burning the house down," Cara said. "I know it was a good victory last night, but there's really no need to riot."

He laughed nervously, as his dad and Piper got the alarm to stop.

"I was wondering if you wanted to hang out tonight," he asked, his heart racing as he said it.

She paused, and took a deep breath. "I can't."

Gael decided right then and there that she hated him, that November was a stupid excuse, and their whole relationship was useless, and—

"But maybe if you want to hang out tomorrow. I'm randomly going to the zoo in Asheboro with a friend, and she said I could bring people if I wanted."

"The zoo?" Gael asked. "Really?"

Piper ran out of the kitchen and was in front of him in seconds.

"The zoo? The zoo? I want to go to the zoo. Take me with you, please please please."

"Chill," Gael said.

"What's that?" Cara asked.

Gael turned away from Piper, as if that might afford him a little privacy.

"My little sister is begging to come." He rolled his eyes. In his *actual* home, Piper wouldn't have been within earshot.

"Oh," Cara said.

Piper kept insisting. "Please please please pretty please."

Gael cleared his throat. "I don't think so—"

"Come on," Piper said. "It will be so much fun! Please please pretty pretty please."

"Uhh, I guess that works," Cara said. "I mean, it would be cool to meet her, anyway."

Gael looked from his sister to his dad, who was nodding eagerly. "All right," Gael said to Piper, resigned. "Looks like we're going to the zoo tomorrow."

Piper immediately did a happy dance.

(So did I.)

team samgael

THE NEXT DAY, PIPER WAS MOSTLY QUIET ON THE FIFTY-three-mile drive to the zoo, which was strange for Piper. She kept pulling out papers from her backpack and looking them over. Gael didn't ask what she was doing. It was usually easier not to ask when it came to Piper.

Instead, he spent the entire time going over and over in his head what Cara must be thinking. She'd said no to a Saturday night hangout and had suggested a super-casual thing with his little sister, no less. Maybe she really did just want to be friends . . .

(Worth noting here is a common little mind trap that you humans frequently fall into: thinking much more about whether the other person likes you than whether *you* actually like *them*.)

Needless to say, Gael was so wrapped up in his thoughts that he was wholly unprepared for what he saw when they finally reached the entrance to the zoo. There, standing right next to Cara, leaning against the entrance to the Africa section, *Candide* in freaking hand . . .

Sammy.

He was so surprised he didn't even think to wave. He turned right down the row of cars, seeking out a spot to park.

"I didn't know Sammy was going to be here!" Piper squealed.

Gael shook his head as he pulled into an open spot. Could Sammy be the "friend" Cara had spoken of? UNC was a school of twenty thousand students—it would be a crazy coincidence. And yet, she must be.

"Believe me," he said to Piper, cursing his luck. "I didn't either."

＊　＊　＊　＊　＊

After the OMG, *I didn't know you were going to be here*s, after Cara explained that Sammy was a friend from school, after Piper yelled at Gael for calling Sammy the "babysitter," not the "French tutor," after all of them marveled at what a small world it was, they purchased their tickets and filed in through the large "Welcome to Africa" plaza.

Piper immediately ran ahead toward the Crocodile Café. The girl was a fiend for slushies.

"Piper," Gael yelled. "You have to wait!"

Sammy broke into a run, grabbed her, and dragged her back to Gael. He instantly felt bad for her—Sammy should not be having to deal with this on her day off. Meanwhile, Cara, who had basically created this awkward mess, gazed at the map like she didn't have a care in the world. He felt a tinge of annoyance, and it surprised him. Cara couldn't have known that her friend was his little sister's babysitter. It was just one of those things. One of those . . . super-strange coincidence things.

Gael turned to Sammy. "You don't have to take care of her. I mean, she's my responsibility today."

"I'm my *own* responsibility." Piper crossed her arms. "Mom said."

Gael cursed his mom for always indulging his little sister's view of the world, and a flash of frustration passed across Sammy's eyes. Still, in that way Sammy had of always putting his sister first, she didn't let Piper see it. Instead, Sammy smiled at her. "Of course you are," Sammy said. "But you still have to stick with the group."

"Fine," Piper said hesitantly. "But I have something fun to show you, so can we hurry up *please?*"

Piper grabbed Gael's and Sammy's hands, dragging them toward the café, while Gael turned to Sammy and mouthed, "Thank you."

Once they'd gotten Piper her bright red slushy and

grabbed a container of sweet potato fries to share, they headed to a table.

Piper immediately pulled two sheets of paper out of her backpack and spread them out proudly on the table.

Gael glanced at the paper. "What's this, Pipes?" he asked.

She beamed. "It's a video scavenger hunt. We divide into teams. I found it on the Internet. Can we do it, please please please?" It all came out in one long Piper breath.

"Uhh, I don't really think—" Cara started.

But Sammy wasn't having it. "You put this whole thing together for us?" she asked Piper.

Piper nodded. "I mean, I just printed it, but I looked on *every* website until I found a good one." (Thanks to my nudging, of course.)

Sammy read off the sheet. "Waddle like a duck for sixty seconds," she said. "A good one, indeed. Should we do it?" Sammy eyed Gael and Cara in a way that showed it was hardly a question.

"Sure," Gael said.

Cara nodded reluctantly.

Gael was with Cara on this one—a video scavenger hunt sounded next-level lame—and yet he couldn't help but appreciate that Sammy took Piper so seriously. He knew Piper loved that.

Piper folded her hands all official-like. "So we split into teams and do all the challenges and videotape the whole thing. And I'm going to be with Cara. We'll be Team Para, like Piper plus Cara, or like paratroopers. See?" She held up one of the sheets. "I already put our name down."

(If you're wondering why Piper didn't want to be with Sammy, allow me to explain. Of course, Piper adored Sammy. But her teacher had given a lesson on the importance of making new friends on Friday—thanks, in large part, to my urgings—and Piper liked to excel at anything her teacher suggested.)

"Are you sure?" Cara asked.

Piper cocked her head to the side. "You don't want to be with me?"

It felt like the world froze. Like the kids in the background temporarily stopped eating their corn dogs, like the middle schooler working the slushy machine was paralyzed. Gael imagined even the giraffes in the distance ceasing to munch on leaves. Like everything stopped as he saw the deep look of hurt on Piper's face.

Piper was an eight-year-old dealing with her parents' divorce and an older brother who hadn't exactly been there for her. She didn't deserve to be hurt further.

Before Gael could try to smooth things over, Sammy swept in. "Don't you want to be with me, Piper?"

A robust man in an Indiana Jones hat scooted past Sammy, and Gael wanted to jump out of his seat, push the guy out of the way, and give Sammy a hug. Here she was on an outing with a friend, and she was willing to sacrifice her whole afternoon just so Piper's feelings wouldn't be hurt.

"Yeah, why don't you do that?" Cara offered. The breeze

from the open-air café messed with her ponytail. She pushed it forcefully back in place. Gael had to stop himself from glaring.

Piper's bottom lip puffed out. "So you really don't want to be on my team?" she asked Cara. "I know a lot about animals, and I'm really good at using the camera on the iPhone."

Cara shrugged.

Gael couldn't take it. "Of course she does." It was one thing for him to tell his little sister to leave him alone, but for an outsider to do that made him, frankly, more than a little annoyed. As much as he'd wanted to spend the day with Cara, it wasn't cool to do so at the expense of his sister's feelings.

"Right," Cara said forcefully. "Yeah. Of course I do."

"So what should *our* team name be?" Sammy asked, trying to change the subject.

"Gammy?" Cara suggested bitterly. "You know, like Team Grandma."

"I guess," Sammy said. She seemed nonplussed with Cara's obvious annoyance. "Gael?"

"Sure," Gael said. By now, he just wanted to get out of the café and on with the silly game. He only prayed that Cara would abandon her bad attitude once she was actually doing the game with his sister.

That's when Piper's eyes lit up. "How about Samgael?"

Sammy giggled immediately. "Samgael Gamgee:

Samwise's black sheep of a cousin, up to his hobbit ears in gambling debts, hits the sauce a bit too much."

Gael couldn't help it. He laughed out loud. Cara, on the other hand, didn't seem to get the joke. No surprise, he supposed, since she didn't exactly like movies.

"I guess it's sort of perfect," Sammy said.

"Yeah," Gael agreed. "I guess it sort of is."

around the world
in three tram stops

THE TEAMS SPLIT UP TO DO THE SCAVENGER HUNT, AND Gael and Sammy hopped on the tram to their agreed-upon beginning point, the Cypress Swamp in North America.

Sammy looked over the sheet as they cruised past elephants chugging along in the distance. "Pretend to be a zoologist doing an important study. Shush anyone who tries to talk. Ooh, and lead the crowd in a rendition of 'I Am the Walrus.' Man, Piper didn't hold back on this one."

Gael laughed. "Piper doesn't hold back on much of anything."

Sammy laughed. "She certainly doesn't, my friend. She certainly doesn't."

Gael fiddled with his jeans pocket. "Thanks for sticking up for her."

Sammy smiled, and it was quiet for a moment between them, with only the sound of children laughing and the *whir-whir* of the bus's hardworking engine.

"So in case you were wondering, I had no idea her friend was you," Gael said. "I wouldn't have tried to rope you into babysitting, I promise."

"I believe you," Sammy said. "Don't worry. We're hardly even friends, really, I just met her yesterday—ooh, look," she squealed, interrupting herself. "There's a baby elephant!"

Gael laughed. "I wouldn't have expected you to go apeshit for baby animals."

Sammy raised an eyebrow. "Name one person with a soul who *doesn't* go apeshit for baby animals. They're, like, animals who are tiny. Who are you, the devil?"

Gael shook his head. "I like them, too. Obviously. But your voice went about a million levels higher just then."

Sammy crossed her arms. "Maybe you should question your ability to maintain an even tone of voice in the face of"—she smiled one of those weird upside-down smiles that little kids do when they're excited—"BABY ELEPHANTS."

The tram turned a corner, and the visions of elephants were replaced by children holding ice-cream bars shaped like zoo animals.

"Anyway," Sammy said, folding her hands in her lap. "Yesterday morning I was making a waffle at the dining hall, and some dick had unscrewed the top on the chocolate chips, and they spilled *everywhere*. Cara helped me clean everything up, and we had breakfast together. She's nice, I guess, though I kind of wanted to strangle her when she was not so nice to Piper."

"I know," Gael said. "It was surprising." And then: "I actually met her in an odd way, too. She hit me out of nowhere on her bike, and then she offered me half her nachos. And then she told me she was going to the zoo with a friend, and here we are. Kind of random, to be honest."

(*twiddles thumbs innocently*)

Sammy nodded. "Yeah, the zoo was my idea. I spend most Sundays with my grandparents, and I wanted a reason to skip at least some of the *Price Is Right* reruns."

"Your grandparents live in Chapel Hill?"

She shook her head. "Just down the road, actually. I come to the enchanting city of Asheboro quite frequently. You have to get creative about finding things to do."

"Damn," Gael said, genuinely surprised. "I call my grandma and grandpa once every two weeks if I'm good."

Actually, since the separation, Gael had barely called his grandparents at all. Every phone conversation had gone from chatting about grades and band to awkwardly asking him, over and over, if he was okay, and how he was handling his parents' split.

Sammy shrugged. "We've always been close, I guess."

Gael stared at her. Even if Sammy's parents split up, she'd probably be just as good a granddaughter. It was just the kind of person she was.

"What?" she asked.

He shifted in his seat. "Nothing," he said. "It's just nice, is all."

"That's me to a tee," she laughed. "Queen of nice!" She pulled her hair back into a tiny bun. "Anyway, this Cara, she's not *the girl* you met on your birthday, is she?"

Gael bit at his lip, suddenly embarrassed. "Yeah."

Sammy laughed, but it sounded a tad forced. "I'm surprised you were willing to be on my team."

Gael looked at her, with her professor-like glasses and her shortish hair and her mouth that could grow twice as large when she was smiling about baby elephants, and suddenly, he didn't mind at all how the day had turned out.

"Nah," he said genuinely. "I'm glad we're on the same team. Even if Samgael is a gambling drunken bastard."

scenes from a north carolina zoo

Clip #1: Length: 0:56

"Please be quiet," Sammy says to an unassuming couple who walks hand in hand by the marsh exhibit, where dragonflies, et al., fly from one lily pad to another. She adjusts her glasses with absolute bravado. "I'm doing a study on the secret language of lily pads. Make a single sound and you'll completely disturb them. There's like a whole entire symphony going on in the water."

The couple miraculously believes her, and the dude even tells his girlfriend to keep it down when she asks Sammy whether she's a researcher from Duke. Gael laughs in the background as Sammy says, matter-of-factly, "They say that Mozart got many of his ideas from the vibrations of lily pads."

Clip #2: Length: 0:33

"I am the *egg man*! They are the *egg men*! I AM THE WALRUS! COO-COO-CA-CHOO!" Gael sings while surrounded by no fewer than five moms and dads and grandpas, who are completely delighted by his song. The camera shakes as Sammy sings along while holding the iPhone. The walrus in the background seems completely nonplussed.

Clip #3: Length: 0:13

Sammy approaches a zoo employee and asks with absolute seriousness, "Excuse me, ma'am, but you can you please point me to the seven-hump wump exhibit?"

Clip #4: Length: 0:19

Gael does his best gorilla impression in front of the ape's sprawling habitat, posturing around on all fours like he was born to walk that way.

"I look ridiculous, don't I?" Gael asks the camera.

"No," Sammy says. "Seriously. You just look awesome."

Clip #5: Length: 0:28

The camera follows Sammy as she walks past grizzly bears and red wolves.

"I believe you're supposed to be waddling like a duck right about now," Gael says in the background.

"I think you should take this one," she says. "I'm wearing a skirt, after all."

"Oh, come on," Gael says, keeping the camera on her.

Sammy places her hands under her chin and bats her eyelashes dramatically. "All right, Mr. Brennan, I'm ready for my close-up,"

Gael zooms in, and her face fills the frame.

"Hey," she says. "Too close!"

Her hand obscures the lens. The video cuts to black.

family dinner for three

AFTER THEY'D WATCHED ALL THE VIDEOS TOGETHER, Gael and Piper said good-bye to Sammy and Cara and headed back to their dad's apartment for one last dinner before going back to their real home for the week.

The second they got in the door, Gael's dad started asking them stupid questions about the zoo without letting up. First, he requested a detailed description from Piper of every freaking exhibit she'd seen. Then, after learning that Piper had arranged the scavenger hunt, he showered them with boatloads of praise all around and demanded to see the videos.

And now, while they were sitting down to family dinner, while Gael was trying with all his might *not* to think about how mind-numbingly strange it still was to be having Sunday dinner in a shitty apartment with the fourth chair at the ugly table conspicuously empty, while all of that was rushing through his head, his dad could not stop asking about the zoo.

"You still haven't answered, Gael. What was your favorite part?" His dad smiled his stupid fake smile and ran a hand through his stupid sandy hair and then cocked his head to the side, waiting.

Of course his dad had cheated, Gael thought. Even Gael could admit he was good-looking for an old guy, with his runner physique and his full head of hair and all that. Once, Gael had read the student reviews on one of those professor-rating sites, and no fewer than three people had complimented Professor Brennan on more than his lecture skills.

That's why his mom was in the house and his dad was in this shithole.

That's why what had seemed so good between his parents had suddenly just . . . *imploded.*

"I'm not, like, eight," Gael spat.

"Hey," Piper said, a bit of turkey chili dripping down her chin. "Eight's a good age."

"It sure is, Pipes," his dad said, taking her chin in his hand and wiping off the mess. He looked to Gael. "And there's no age too old to enjoy something like the zoo."

Gael set his spoon down. "Well, then maybe you should take her next time. Maybe we should all go together, like we used to. Oh wait, we can't."

His dad shook his head and looked down at his bowl, but Piper just scrunched her eyebrows. "Why can't we?" she asked genuinely.

"Because Mom and Dad aren't together anymore," Gael said. "When are you going to get that through your head?"

Piper's bottom lip puffed out, and her eyes began to water.

"Gael," his dad snapped. "Stop it."

Gael scooted out of his chair and stood up. "What? Both you and Mom have totally misled her. She thinks this is just all going back to normal once you guys make up. Well, you're not going to, that's obvious, and she might as well know that."

"Yes they will!" Piper yelled. "You don't know anything!" She seethed as she looked at him. "I hate you!"

Gael felt her words deep in his gut. His dad rushed to console Piper, but Gael wasn't going to let him off the hook.

"I didn't do this. *You* did," Gael said, and then he stomped out of the room and to the bathroom, slamming the door behind him.

Gael, in his anger, was desperate for some confirmation, for further proof. He began to rifle through all two of the bathroom's cabinets, under the sink, and in the shower. He wanted something that would prove his theory. Maybe he'd find the girl's brush or razor, like in a movie. Or a pot of lip gloss or . . . or something.

Finally, after a second examination of the medicine cabinet, his eyes caught a flash of pink behind the Advil.

Gael moved the bottles out of the way. A hot pink toothbrush. A ladies' one, no doubt. With a nice little case covering the top part. He pulled it out and popped open the case. It wasn't dry as a bone. It had been used, and recently.

His dad's toothbrush was electric, and it was sitting on the counter, next to Gael's and Piper's.

Between the phone calls and the bullshit "office hours"

and this, there was no way Gael could deny it. His dad had cheated on his mom. His dad was having an affair.

Still, as much as he wanted to, Gael couldn't bring himself to run back in the room and confront his dad, not in front of Piper. She didn't deserve more pain, even if his dad did.

And so Gael went back to his stupid room and slammed the stupid door and tried not to listen to the sound of Piper crying through the stupid thin walls.

clueless

ON A SCALE OF EVERYTHING'S AWFUL TO NOT SO BAD
At All, Gael was definitely leaning toward the former by
the end of school on Monday. Between his fight with his
dad and Piper and the discovery of the toothbrush, any
remotely happy feelings from the weekend had completely
disappeared. On Sunday night, he'd apologized to Piper (but
not to his dad—he didn't think his dad deserved much of
anything these days), and around nine they'd driven back
home.

He and Cara had made plans to grab coffee after her
last class on Monday. It was the one thing that had gotten
him through the day—he'd even caved and agreed to go to
Starbucks to please her. He didn't care if she'd been a little
annoying at the zoo. He needed her now more than ever.

But after school, as he pulled up to his house that afternoon, he got a text from Cara:

last-minute group project, can we reschedule?

Gael looked at the clock on his dash. It was 3:20 P.M.
They were supposed to get coffee at 3:30. Last minute,
indeed.

He wrote back: *sure, tomorrow?*

He watched as she typed her reply. Paused. Typed again.

(The beautiful irony was, I'd planned on manufacturing a reason to prevent Cara from going, but she beat me to it. Frankly, she was still a little pissed at him. Her idea had been to invite him along with her new friend to slow it down a bit so she could keep her October vow, not to babysit Gael's kid sister while he hung out with another girl. Cara didn't even like kids that much. She'd only invited Gael's sister because she'd felt bad.)

Finally:

tomorrow's no good, either, got work til the weekend pretty much

Gael hesitated. Was she blowing him off? Was this it? The logical part of his mind told him yes.

But another part (the Romantic part) thought about their kiss and the way they'd looked at each other at the basketball game, and he decided to take it all in stride. He typed quickly, before he could lose his nerve:

i know you don't love movies but how about making an exception for the new Wes Anderson on Friday?

If he was going to make it work with this girl, he was going to have to expand her movie knowledge beyond James Cameron, after all.

The part of Cara that wasn't pissed (the Serial Monogamist part) replied: *yes.*

Gael tucked his phone back in his pocket and got out of the car. He headed for the front door and paused. He was worn out from the argument with his dad, stressed from lunchtime woes, and the thought of sitting alone in his room seemed torturous. He didn't even really want to watch a movie.

Gael turned around and headed back to the car. He needed to do something instead of just sitting around and moping. He opened the car and clicked the garage door opener.

The garage was still full of his dad's things. A shelf of ceramic pots from the time his dad had decided to take a pottery class. Tools that his mom used more than he did. An old jacket from college, which he only used for mowing the lawn. A tennis ball hung perfectly so his dad's Subaru would fit just right, which was no longer necessary with his mom's little smart car. It was like this part of the house simply hadn't been informed of the news.

Gael headed to the back and grabbed the rake, then walked to the front yard and began to tackle the leaves.

It had always been his dad's job, raking the leaves. Gael remembered the one time his mom had decided that their chore division was too "gendered" and had taken it over. It wasn't three days before she came into the house, handed his dad the rake, and said: "If traditional gender roles mean I never have to rake leaves again, I'll take it." His dad had just laughed and kissed her on the cheek, before taking the rake and finishing the backyard.

He probably should have done this sooner, Gael thought, as he gathered the leaves into a big pile, his arms beginning to ache in a way that felt good. He probably shouldn't have been so obsessed with his own drama and been there a little bit more for his mom.

He was about halfway done when Sammy came outside.

She put a hand on her hip. He stopped, planting the rake in the ground like the bald guy from that famous painting.

Sammy smiled, surveying the work. "Nice raking."

Gael shrugged. "I thought I might as well do something with my wide open afternoons, besides driving you and Piper nuts."

Sammy laughed. "Well, speaking of, Piper sent me out here to inform you, in no uncertain terms, that she's still very mad at you."

Gael sighed. Even though he'd apologized, he knew he'd hurt Piper. But he didn't know exactly what to do. It was the kind of hurt that he couldn't fix. Because she might be mad at him right now, but she was really mad at the words he'd said, and those words were the truth. No apology would change that.

"What happened?" Sammy asked. "It's not really like Piper to be mad at people."

"I yelled at her a little bit," he said, embarrassed. "I mean, not really *at* her, but I yelled anyway. She's somehow got the idea in her head that my parents are going to get back together, and neither of them are exactly disabusing her of that notion."

Sammy let her arms fall to her sides. "That sucks," she

said. "My parents split up when I was about Piper's age. It's hard to grasp, for sure."

Gael had an overwhelming urge to put his arms around her, hold her tight, but he pushed the thought away. "I'm sorry," he said. "I didn't know that."

Sammy kicked a leaf back that had been blown out of his neat pile. "It's been awhile. I've processed it. I just know how hard it is, especially when you're young."

Gael set the rake down and sat in the perfect patch of grass he'd just cleared. "Sit down for a second," he said casually, thinking how easy it was to just be himself around her. "Ditch your babysitting duties."

Sammy raised an eyebrow. "I take babysitting duty very seriously, as I'm sure you know." But then she smiled and sat down across from him.

Gael picked up a leaf and started ripping it into bits. Then he sat back and stretched.

"Why did your parents split up?" he asked. "If you don't mind me asking."

She shrugged, grabbed a handful of leaves, and tossed them up. They spun around as they fell back down. Sammy tucked her hair behind her ears and spread out her fingers in the grass. "I don't even know," she said. "They just did."

Gael looked up at the sky, and his dad's motto accosted him, like it often did on a bright sunny day—"If God isn't a Tar Heel, why is the sky Carolina blue?" He pushed his dad's chipper voice out of his head. Then he looked back at Sammy. She was wearing a black jumper and a striped top underneath, and her short hair was pulled up into a knot like some kind of chic French ballet dancer. He imagined her twirling around in the raked leaves, kicking them up and turning it all messy again.

He decided in that moment that he trusted her with this. "I think my dad cheated on my mom," he said.

Sammy sat up straight and adjusted her glasses. "*Really?*"

"You're surprised?" he asked.

"Why do you think that? Your dad doesn't seem like that kind of guy at all."

Gael shrugged, but her reaction weakened his resolve. She didn't have to look *so* shocked. It wasn't that crazy of an idea. Sure, he'd always thought of his dad as a generally nice guy, but nice people did shitty things all the time. Look at Anika and Mason.

"There has to be some reason. It's the only thing that makes sense."

Sammy looked down at her hands. "There doesn't always have to be a big *groundbreaking* reason," she said. "Sometimes it's just a bunch of little reasons."

Gael stared at her, incredulous.

He looked up at the sky, wishing he could believe her. But it seemed like in his life, there was always a big reason. Finally, he looked back to her.

"You know, you're kind of an inspiration," he said, eager to move the subject away from his parents.

Sammy laughed, turned her head ever so slightly to the side. "What do you mean?"

He shrugged. "You and John. It's been three years, right? And you're both in college and you're still making it work."

(Face palm.)

Sammy forced a smile. "I guess," she said.

She stood up. "I really should get back to Piper. Good luck on the rest of the leaves."

Gael watched her go in, completely unaware of what had just happened.

intervention

THE NEXT DAY AT SCHOOL, GAEL WAS SHOCKED TO SEE Anika and Mason back at their old spots at the lunch table.

He stopped short. He did not need to deal with them right now. He had more than enough to process between Piper being angry, the discoveries about his dad, and his worries that Cara was already growing tired of him.

Of course, he could leave it to those two to know exactly how to kick him when he was down.

I feel a little bad even admitting this, but I didn't try to stop them this time. I had watched, the night before, as Gael stared at his phone, desperately wanting to call the one person he'd relied on more than anyone when his parents were splitting up, the one person who'd been content to listen to him gripe and wonder and try to make sense of it all. He wanted to call Anika.

With my nudgings, coupled with his own resolve, he'd talked himself out of it. But still, he'd wanted to.

A little reminder that Anika was no longer in his corner wouldn't hurt.

Okay, it would hurt, actually. Pretty badly. But sometimes hurt is necessary. It's just an unfortunate reality of my job.

Anika smiled at Gael like nothing was the matter. Danny and Jenna were wearing fake, forced smiles of their own. Mason was the only one who avoided his eyes.

"Umm," Gael said. "What are you doing?"

"We thought we'd join you guys for lunch. That's cool, right?" Anika asked.

Anika had always been good at asking questions that weren't really questions at all.

Gael crossed his arms. He looked to Mason, who was just staring at the table. "Umm, no, obviously that's not cool."

Anika sighed. "We were talking, and—"

"Who's *we*?" Gael demanded.

Jenna cleared her throat and held Danny's hand in hers. "Look, Gael, we get that you're really hurt, and you totally have a right to be. But it's not really fair to the group, you know? I mean, we're all friends, and Danny and I didn't do anything. And it has been more than a week of sitting apart. So we were thinking we could all start sitting together again."

Gael scoffed. "Are you guys freaking kidding me? What, did you have like a team meeting about this without me?"

Danny squeezed Jenna's hand. "We think you should come back to marching band, too," Danny said. "We miss you in the sax section."

Gael rolled his eyes. "Too late. Mr. Potter told me on Friday that I missed too many practices now to come back this semester. Such a shame, I really wish I could spend more time with all of you guys, together again." Even Gael was surprised by the level of bitterness in his voice. There was silence for a moment.

"We're just worried about you, Gael," Anika said timidly. "We think it would be better if we were all friends again."

Gael laughed, but underneath it, he felt like he might break down. It was one thing to deal with Mason's awkward attempts at reconciliation. It was another to sit here, day in and day out, and pretend that everything was the same.

"If that's what you all want, I'll just eat by myself," he said finally. He turned to head back out to his old trusty courtyard. It was pretty cold out today, but it didn't matter. It was better than this.

And that's what finally broke Mason's stoicism. "No," he said. "No, that's not what I want at all." He glared at Anika. "I told you this was a bad idea. Come on, we'll go back to our table."

Anika humphed. "*Mason*. I only agreed to change seats because I thought it would be *temporary*."

"Whatever. I'm not doing this," Mason snapped. And he pushed his chair out, the legs making an awful screeching sound, and walked away.

Anika sighed loudly, then followed him back to their table in the corner.

"Thanks a lot, guys," Gael snapped, taking his usual seat and angrily pulling out his sandwich.

"It was Anika's idea," Danny said.

Jenna smacked him on the arm.

He shrugged. "Well, it was."

Gael took a bite of his sandwich, but his eyes drifted toward Anika and Mason, where they sat with their backs to him.

Mason might be the worst best friend in the history of best friends, Gael thought, but it was nice to know that at least he hadn't turned into a *total* lunatic.

rom-coms, an education

THAT AFTERNOON, GAEL APPROACHED HIS HOUSE AT HIS usual early, marching-band-free time.

What Gael had said at today's quasi-intervention was true. Mr. Potter wasn't going to let him back in until the following semester. Plus, he wasn't sure he wanted to go back. At least, not yet, anyway.

When he got inside, he saw Sammy sitting at the dining room table, arms crossed, eyebrows knit. She was surrounded by scraps of tulle and satin from the elaborate Marie Antoinette costume his mom was making for Piper for Halloween, and she was tracing circles with her finger in the ivory tablecloth.

"Do you know where Piper is?" Sammy asked. "She should have been here fifteen minutes ago. I'm getting worried."

It took Gael a minute to put it together. "Oh shit," Gael said. "I think she has a field trip." He remembered Piper saying something about the UNC planetarium over breakfast. It was the first time she'd sounded more like her usual self, like she wasn't mad at him anymore. "My mom didn't call you?"

Sammy glanced at her phone. "Nope, no missed calls. Looks like she forgot to tell me."

Gael shrugged. It would have been nuts for his mom to miss a detail like that months ago, but now? Not so much. "Sorry you had to come for nothing."

Sammy sighed. "It's fine." She grabbed her bag and slung it over her shoulder, standing up. "I'll see you tomorrow, I guess."

As she headed for the door, Gael followed her. "Wait," he said.

Sammy turned back, exasperated. "Yeah?" she asked.

Gael wanted to ask her why she'd walked away so abruptly yesterday. He wanted to ask her if everything was all right. But suddenly it seemed ridiculous—pushy. "You want to hang out or something?" he asked. "Since you're already here?"

Sammy shrugged, then adjusted her glasses. "What do you want to do?"

His eyes searched the room for some kind of idea and landed on his mom's *Entertainment Weekly*. "Uhh, we could go to a movie? I'm not sure what's out, the new Wes Anderson doesn't open until Friday, not that you would want to see that, but we could walk down to the Varsity and see what's playing."

Just then, the *Entertainment Weekly* fluttered off the dining room table, landing at Sammy's feet. Gael glanced at the open window. *Weird,* he thought. He could have sworn that was closed a minute ago.

(I mean, I have no earthly idea how that window got open, either. *winks*)

Sammy picked it up. "I totally forgot that *Goodbye Yesterday* was out. That's playing at the Varsity."

Gael raised an eyebrow, stepping closer to see the spread. A generically good-looking girl looked up at a tall, lanky guy. "A romantic comedy," he laughed. "Of course."

Sammy rolled her eyes. "Well, the only other option at the Varsity is likely some depressing foreign film. They're always playing that kind of thing."

Gael burst into laughter. "Are you serious?"

Sammy crossed her arms and leaned back against the front door. "Watching foreign movies that aren't assigned for class feels like work. Plus, *Goodbye Yesterday* is by a seriously funny woman with an awesome YouTube series. It's not going to be as cheesy as you think. And even if it is, one cheesy movie won't kill you."

She pulled out her phone and tapped a few times. "It's playing in half an hour. If we leave now, we'll just make it."

"All right, all right," Gael said, throwing his hands into the air. "But I reserve the right to ceaselessly criticize it afterward."

Sammy smirked. "Maybe you won't even want to."

"Maybe." Gael grabbed some money from his mom's emergency canister on the kitchen counter (he thought it only seemed right since she'd forgotten to cancel on Sammy), shrugged into his jacket, and followed Sammy out the door.

There was a chill in the air as they headed down Henderson Street toward Franklin. Sammy wrapped an intricately patterned scarf around her neck and shoved her hands deep in her pockets.

"So are you telling me you mostly watch rom-coms?" Gael asked.

Sammy shrugged. "I do watch a lot of them, but I mostly watch horror, to be totally honest."

"*Really?*" he asked.

"Yeah," she said. "You got a problem with that, too?"

Gael shook his head. "It just seems so unlike you."

They cut over to Rosemary Street as a car blasting Sublime flew past them.

"Look, I watch all the serious movies, too. But if you're going to be a genre snob, you're going to miss out on a lot of good stuff. What's your deal *against* romantic comedies, anyway?" she asked.

"My deal," Gael said, as stunning Southern homes and the occasional frat house rose up around them, "is that they're really formulaic, and the writing is always bad, and they're so . . . *predictable.*"

Sammy smirked. "Oh, and the movies you like are so much better? I've seen the shelves in your room. Seventies crime movies. *Eternal Sunshine of the Spotless Mind.* Wes Anderson. Don't tell me Wes Anderson isn't super predictable. A young boy struggles to find his place in the world, and the girls are all quirky, and the colors look way more vivid than they do in real life!"

Gael laughed. "Hey, his movies are so fun to watch."

Sammy crossed her arms defiantly. "So are romantic comedies. There's nothing wrong with genre movies."

Gael rolled his eyes. "All right, so some movies I like are a little predictable. But you can't seriously argue that movies like *Serpico* and *Taxi Driver* are basic. They're *epic*."

"Ooh well, I actually like *Serpico*," she said, as they waited to cross the street. "But let me do it anyway: Young guy tries to beat all the bad guys, gets in over his head, caves under the pressure, messes up his love life, but still wins in the end!"

Gael ignored her rather sound argument as a car stopped, letting them cross. "None of my friends have even heard of *Serpico*, much less seen it."

Sammy shrugged. "My dad is from Brooklyn, and he's like *obsessed* with movies that were made in New York during that time—he's always saying that the seventies were the last time that New York was really New York, even though he was like eight years old then and my grandma talks about how she could never take him to the park because of all the drug needles lying around."

"Wow," Gael said. "I can't imagine growing up in Brooklyn. That's so cool."

The two of them cut down the alleyway between Rosemary and Franklin Street, the same alleyway where the flower lady had told Gael, not even two weeks ago, that Anika wasn't worth it. Gael wanted to laugh out loud at the memory. Who knew that flower sellers were so wise?

"All right," Gael continued. "Do *Eternal Sunshine*, then," he said. "You can't very well say that's predictable."

Sammy bit her lip.

"What?" he asked.

"I haven't exactly seen it."

Gael stopped in his tracks right in the middle of the alley. "Are you kidding me?"

Sammy put a hand on her hip. "It's like anyone who thinks they're a movie person *loves* that movie. It can't be *that* good. I read the description. It sounds awful."

"Just watch it," Gael said.

"Yeah, yeah."

"I'm serious. I am not moving from this dank alleyway until you promise you'll watch it."

She started to walk ahead, but he didn't budge.

She walked about ten feet before she realized he wasn't behind her. She turned back to him. "Really?" She put a hand on her hip.

He put one on his, too. Mocking. But the nice kind of mocking. "I told you I'm not moving. If you want to go to the movie by yourself, go right ahead."

Sammy took one step closer. "Are you seriously holding me hostage with what's probably an overhyped hipster movie?"

He nodded. "Oh, believe me, I am."

She paused, assessing him. Then her face broke into a smile. "All right," she said, lifting one hand in the air. "Promise."

"Was that so hard?" he asked, running to catch up to her.

The two of them emerged onto Franklin.

"If I watch *Eternal Sunshine*, you owe me one of my choice," Sammy argued, as they got into line behind four other people.

"Isn't *this* your choice?"

Sammy rolled her eyes. She was good at that. "This is what I picked because it was playing at the right time—and really, I think it's going to be good. But it's not, like, *the movie* I want you to see. Get your hands on *When Harry Met Sally*. Believe me."

The people in front of them finished paying and stepped aside.

"Can I help you?" The ticket taker had two eyebrow piercings and a tattoo of the jack of spades peeking from beneath his black T-shirt. He looked particularly macabre behind the cobweb-decorated box office window.

"Two for *Goodbye Yesterday*," Gael said. He glanced over at Sammy as the guy handed him the tickets: "I hear it's a good one."

a brief peek into mason's world

WHILE SAMMY AND GAEL WERE WATCHING THE LOVE interest of *Goodbye Yesterday* make his inevitable grand gesture to get back the girl, Mason was busy working on a grand gesture of his own.

He'd canceled plans with Anika and headed to the craft store for poster board and supplies.

Now he was sitting at the dining room table, a forkful of his mom's leftover fettuccine alfredo in one hand and a glue stick in the other.

He meticulously researched each element. He drudged through a mire of Wikipedia articles without any of them really sinking in. He, for once all year, actually did the assigned chemistry reading.

He clipped and glued and wrote in fine-tip Sharpie.

He didn't care how long it took. He didn't care if he had to stay up all night.

He was determined to do something—anything—to finally make this better.

and the truth finally comes out

IT WAS DARK WHEN GAEL AND SAMMY LEFT THE THEATER, the street lamps on, casting a glow upon the kids in line for Coldstone and the students coming out of the T-shirt shop with gear for the weekend's big football game. They walked lazily, meandering past each brick storefront, past Krispy Kreme and Sutton's, the old-fashioned pharmacy that sold malted milkshakes and had barely changed since the fifties.

"So was it as brutal as you imagined?" Sammy asked.

Gael slowed down as they approached the post office, where he used to hang out in what seemed like a whole other world. "I have to say, it was actually kind of good."

Sammy punched him on the shoulder. "See? I told you! Wasn't the dialogue great?" Her hand drifted back to her side. "And how about the camera work? I bet you weren't expecting that."

Gael shook his head. "I can absolutely guarantee you I wasn't."

A group of ultra-pierced pseudo-punks holding Frappuccino cups walked past them, and Sammy turned toward UNC's North Campus. Gael followed her gaze toward the tall, mostly leafless trees, and the diagonal brick sidewalks, and the planetarium where he and Anika had kissed, and Linda's, a bar that Gael's parents used to go to sometimes. This town held so much history. It reminded him of how quickly everything could change.

She looked back to him. "I guess I should head back to my dorm," she said.

Gael paused, and I gave him just the *tiniest* idea.

"You should definitely get back. You wouldn't want John thinking this was a date or anything." He smiled.

But Sammy didn't smile back. Her face instantly fell flat.

"Sorry," he said. "Stupid dad joke. Apologies."

But Sammy was shaking her head. She looked down at her scuffed black boots and then back up at him. "It's not your fault. It's just that I haven't been totally honest with you."

Gael felt a weight descend in his stomach. Maybe she was lying yesterday, when she said she didn't think his dad would cheat. Maybe she even knew something that he didn't . . .

His eyes drifted to Linda's again, and he wondered if his dad had taken that girl there, too. "Just tell me," he said finally.

She narrowed her eyes at him. "It's not anything bad. I mean, it is, but it's not anything bad for you. It's just that . . . well . . ."

"What?" Gael asked.

She bit her lip. "I feel so stupid saying this and I honestly don't know why it's so hard. Okay." She took a deep breath. "It's just that John and I broke up a month and a half ago."

Gael whipped his head back. "Whoa," he said. "I was *not* expecting that."

She shrugged. "I know. I should have said something sooner."

A crowd of students walked past them, and Gael stepped to the side. She followed him. "Why didn't you?"

Sammy glanced around before answering, as if looking for an out. "I don't know. You and your mom still seemed pretty shook up from what happened with your parents, and it just seemed not very important in comparison. And then I was going to say something—I even tried to mention it that night at your birthday—but you had so much else on your mind." She paused for breath. "And then it had just been so long, and of course you guys just assumed that we were still together, and I don't know, it just felt weirder and weirder to say something out of the blue."

"Geez," he said. "What happened?"

Sammy looked away. "He basically said that he needed to 'find' himself in his new school." Sammy made the appropriate air quotes. "Which I'm pretty sure is just code for hook up with other people. I should have seen it coming. I should have realized that we'd be like everyone else, that there was no way we'd make it through college long distance."

Gael frowned.

(So did I. Sure, Sammy might like rom-coms, which

she felt were about as believable as her other favorite, horror movies, but when it came to real life, she was a Cynic[5] through and through. The whole time she'd been dating John she'd just been waiting for something to go wrong. I hated that, in the end, it had. It wasn't always going to be that way, of course—there was lots of good in store for her—but Cynics are always hard to convince.)

"I promise I'm not one of those like weird stalkers who refuses to accept their breakup," Sammy said nervously.

Gael laughed out loud at that. "I wouldn't think that," he said. "I just feel like such a dick. I was going on and on about how you couldn't possibly understand and, god, yesterday when I said you were my relationship inspiration. You knew *exactly* what I was going through."

He felt like an idiot. He should have seen the truth. Even if Sammy hadn't said it outright, he should have known somehow.

Sammy shook her head. "Don't worry. It was my fault. But to answer your question, no, John won't be jealous. And now I really should go."

And before he could say another word, she turned on her heel and sauntered across the crosswalk, just making

---

5. Cynic: One who refuses to buy a single thing that the movies, their friends, or even their lovey-dovey grandparents have told them about romance. Believes that most relationships are doomed to fail and thus tries to protect themselves when they find themselves in one. May result in holding back from expressing true feelings, expecting things to go wrong, and waiting for the other shoe to drop. May also lead to amazing loyalty once they do let someone in because they do it so infrequently.

it before the green light turned red. Gael watched her walk down the path into the campus until he couldn't see her anymore.

And then he turned up Henderson, heading toward home, and for some reason, his steps were just the tiniest bit lighter.

true bromance

FOR THE FIRST TIME IN A LONG TIME, GAEL WAS ACTUALLY in an okay mood at school the next day.

Piper was no longer mad at him, lunch was back to being Anika-free, and he was excited that he was going to see Sammy again that afternoon. Last night, he'd managed to squeeze in Sammy's movie rec after his mom had ordered pizza and they'd binged on some Piper-appropriate TV. He'd lost a good bit of sleep just so he could watch *When Harry Met Sally*, and he couldn't wait to talk to her about it.

But when Gael got to fifth-period chemistry, Mason was not only early (completely unlike him), but he had a huge grin on his face. He looked like he seriously wanted to talk. There went Gael's mood.

Gael threw his backpack onto the chemistry table and tried to ignore him. Whatever Mason's grin meant, he was sure it would be annoying. Maybe instead of begging for advice about Anika, he wanted to share some new exciting development in their relationship. *Umm, no thanks.*

Mason turned to face him, grin still intact.

Gael pulled his big brick of a book out of his bag but didn't indulge Mason. Yes, he'd stuck up for Gael yesterday, but that didn't suddenly mean they were best buddies again, even if Gael *was* in a particularly good mood.

"Uh-uhm," Mason cleared his throat.

Gael didn't turn his head.

"UH-UHM."

"You're not going to stop doing that until I talk to you, are you?" Gael asked.

In response, Mason pushed a colorful piece of poster board his way.

Gael glanced down. "What's this?"

Mason beamed. "It's the extra-credit project. A whole extra three points on our end-of-semester grades, enough to keep me out of C territory and you at a solid A." Mason pointed to the names at the top right corner: *Gael Brennan and Mason Dewart, 5th Period.*

"You didn't have to do that," Gael said, confused. "You should cross my name out. I didn't do anything."

Mason shrugged. "It's the same credit either way. Take it, dude. Plus, I already wrote your name in Sharpie. It would look shady if I crossed it out now."

Gael surveyed the work. Surprisingly, it looked pretty good.

"We had to pick ten different elements or elemental compounds and illustrate their uses in real life," Mason said matter-of-factly, as if he'd even known what any of those things were a week ago.

"I don't even remember Mrs. Ellison talking about this," Gael said.

Mason laughed as he ran his finger along the bottom of the poster board. "You haven't exactly been paying a ton of attention."

Gael raised an eyebrow, but Mason threw up his hands. "I know, I know," he said. "With perfectly good reason."

Gael shook his head as he looked over the sheet. "Kr is Krypton, dude, not Kryptoni*te*."

"Oh, shit, sorry," Mason said.

"Just give me your pen," Gael said with a laugh. He crossed out the extra letters as cleanly as possible.

"So you approve?" Mason asked. "I can turn it in?"

"Yes," Gael said, after a moment. "I approve."

Mason shot out of his seat and walked to the front, where he set the poster board on top of a couple of other people's extra-credit projects on Mrs. Ellison's desk.

Gael waited until Mason was back in his seat. "Oh, and thanks, by the way," he said quickly. Then he whipped his chemistry book open and pretended to read it as fast as he could.

But he couldn't help but hand it to his friend. Correction—*former* friend. He might be a shameless, lying scumbag, but he had done a pretty nice thing.

What can I say? Sometimes, the best grand gestures of love don't have anything to do with romance at all.

missed wes connection

PIPER WAS IN FINE FORM THAT AFTERNOON, IN ANTICIPA-tion of Halloween and her completely over-the-top cos-tume (he had to give his mom props—she could go through a divorce *and* create a truly magnificent eighteenth-century costume, all while holding down a job and gener-ally keeping it all together). Piper demanded that Sammy give her a special lesson on Marie Antoinette, complete with phrases like "*Qu'ils mangent de la brioche.*" Apart from frequent walk-bys to see if they were done, Gael mainly left them to themselves because Piper had asked him to not interrupt their "important work." Gael was still trying to earn Piper points after his unfortunate outburst at din-ner on Sunday.

In fact, it was nearly 5:00 when Gael finally saw Piper working quietly while Sammy read *Candide*.

"I watched *When Harry Met Sally* last night," Gael blurted out.

Sammy startled, then looked up and laughed.

Perhaps he should have tried a better opener.

"Sorry, I was just excited," he said.

Piper crossed her arms. "I'm trying to learn things. Do you have to talk?"

Sammy looked down at Piper. "If you want quiet space, you know you can always go into the living room," she said.

Piper humphed and stayed put.

"And?" Sammy asked.

Gael winced. "I gotta say, it was kind of contrived."

She laughed loudly. "So you were just eager to tell me that I have terrible taste in movies?" She leaned back in her chair at the dining room table, folded her hands in her lap. Gael pulled a seat out for himself and joined her.

"I didn't say it was bad," Gael argued. "But why wouldn't they have gotten together in all those years? It makes no sense. Obviously just a way to draw the movie out."

"But the dialogue!" Sammy exclaimed. "Nora Ephron's writing is so smart!"

"The whole *let's take forever to be together* thing just really got me," he said.

Sammy rolled her eyes. "But that's the point! Sometimes the right people are always getting the timing wrong."

Piper looked up: "Yeah, sometimes people don't even realize they like each other."

(Here here, Piper!)

Gael ignored her. "I thought you said that timing was everything, that sometimes it just doesn't work out," he chided Sammy.

She crossed her arms. "Well, I guess sometimes it actually does. Anyway," she said. "I *may* have skipped my French reading to stay up and watch *Eternal Sunshine*."

"Did you like it?" Gael asked.

Sammy took a deep breath. She pressed her lips together, suddenly serious. "I'm sorry I ever doubted you, Gael Brennan."

Gael burst into a grin. "Isn't it *amazing*?"

"The scene with the rain in the living room. And when they break into the house. And when he's a little boy again. And Clementine's amazing one-liners." She stopped for breath. "I never should have underestimated it."

Gael shrugged. "What can I say? I have good taste."

Sammy ran her fingers through her hair. "Totally. And I'm supposed to watch *Being John Malkovich* next?"

Gael nodded. "You have to. And report back."

That's when his mom walked in the door.

"Mom!" Piper called, rushing up to her before she could so much as put her purse down. "You have to hear everything I learned about Marie Antoinette!"

His mom leaned down and gave Piper a kiss on the cheek and then stood up, gazing at Gael and Sammy with a funny look in her eyes.

Sammy scooted out of her chair and stood up. "I guess I should be going. Gael, weren't you going to show me that thing outside?"

"Huh?" Gael said.

Sammy raised her eyebrows.

"Oh," he said, standing up quickly. "Yeah. *That* thing."

Both his mom and Piper sported matching smirks, but Gael ignored them.

He followed Sammy out the door, taking in her oversize

button-down, shorts over tights, what looked like a backpack from her dad's college days, and lace-up red boots. Anika would be horrified by how little her clothes matched. Cara would probably wonder why anyone would wear shoes less comfortable than Birks. And yet, for Sammy, it worked somehow.

Gael shut the front door behind them, and Sammy turned around to face him.

It was almost dark, the sun setting, turning the sky a purple color that matched Sammy's eye shadow.

She tugged at the bottom of her shorts with one hand, then looked up at him. "Sorry for being awkward." She laughed. "I just wanted to talk to you without the whole Brennan brigade in tow."

Gael hesitated, wondering what she was going to say.

"I guess I just still felt a little weird for lying to you about John. I don't want you to think I'm some freak who can't face reality or something."

Gael shook his head quickly. "I didn't. At all. And if anyone can't face reality, it's me. You saw me the week after Anika dumped me."

"Well, it's been a little longer for me," she said playfully. Then she averted her eyes to a point about five inches to the left of Gael's head. "But anyway, as long as you don't think I'm insane, I was wondering if you maybe wanted to see the new Wes Anderson this weekend? I *know* I already teased you about him, but A, as you may have guessed, I kind of like to go against the grain with pop culture, and B, well, I *do* owe you something in your genre of choice, even if the genre is whimsical male fantasies . . ."

(Sammy's eyes being on that point five inches to the left of Gael's head, a tiny chip in the exterior paint, to be exact, she couldn't see the progression of Gael's emotions as I could. She couldn't see the way his eyes lit up when she started to ask him to hang out, and the way they instantly clouded when she said Wes Anderson. Instead, by the time she did venture a look, she only saw the sour expression of someone conflicted.)

"I mean, you don't have to, really. I'd probably hate the movie, anyway," she said, trying to save face.

"No," he said. "It's not that I don't want to . . . it's just that I already asked Cara if she wanted to go see it with me on Friday."

Sammy pressed her lips together for the tiniest of seconds. Then she broke into a smile. "Oh yeah, of course. I guess I kind of forgot you guys were a thing—"

"We're not really—"

"—and I forgot Friday is usually date night. I've been out of the game a little too long, I guess."

"It's not exactly—"

But Sammy didn't let him finish.

"I really should be going. I still have to catch up on that French reading." She walked away briskly.

Gael felt like a bit of an ass, but he didn't have time to fully process what had just happened, because as soon as he got back inside, his mom and Piper were waiting eagerly.

"What was that about?" his mom asked.

"What?" he said.

Piper wiggled her shoulders and batted her eyelashes. "Ooh, Gael, can you show me something outside?"

She and his mom both burst into giggles.

Gael sighed. "I don't know what you're talking about," he said.

His mom pursed her lips. "So what did you show her, then?"

"Nothing." Gael pushed past them, nonplussed.

He didn't want to talk about Sammy with them. He didn't want his every move to be on display. Nothing was even happening between them, and yet his mom was already freaking out. Imagine if something did.

And then imagine if it didn't work out? The whole thing would be a total disaster, Gael was sure of it.

It had been bad enough that his mom had become friendly with Anika. There would have been no surprise appearances at birthday dinners if he'd properly compartmentalized his life.

He thought about Cara, how safe she was. How his parents didn't even so much as know her name.

Maybe it wasn't so bad that Cara was the one he was going to see the movie with after all.

clueless: part two

"ANY PLANS TONIGHT, DUDE?" DANNY ASKED AT LUNCH on Friday.

Gael almost choked on his turkey sandwich. He hadn't had "plans" with any of the old group since everything had so suddenly gone down.

Jenna didn't wait for a response. "We're going to a party at Amberleigh's house. Apparently she's, like, trying to befriend the rest of the band now"—Jenna rolled her eyes—"whatever, but it sounds like her parents' house is sick, and they're chill." She raised a hand to stop any objection he might have. "Don't worry. Anika and Mason aren't going."

Gael swallowed and took a sip of Dr Pepper. "I can't. I have . . . err . . . *plans*."

The shocked look on both Danny's and Jenna's faces was insulting, to say the least.

"I do have other friends, you know."

They both laughed at that.

"I do," Gael asserted. "It wasn't a joke."

"I know, I know," Danny said. "But the way you said it was funny. So what are you doing?"

Jenna smirked, then turned to Danny, delighted. "He's going out with a girl."

Gael shook his head. "How in the world—"

She ticked off the points on her fingers. "Your face just got red. You're acting totally weird about your quote-unquote plans. And I hate to break it to you, but we pretty much know all your friends. At least the ones good enough to have *plans* with."

"Wait," Danny said. "Is it your sister's babysitter?"

And then Gael *did* choke on his sandwich.

(That one wasn't even me, I'll have you know.)

Danny patted him on the back, but Gael held up his hand to stop him. "I'm fine." He drank the rest of the Dr Pepper. "But where did you get that idea?"

"Mason says she's hot," Danny said. Jenna immediately smacked him on the arm.

"What?" he asked.

"Why are you talking about other girls being hot?" She pouted.

"So I'm not allowed to ever think another girl is hot again?"

"Guys," Gael said, interrupting them. "It's not her. It's this girl I met on my birthday, and her name is Cara, and we're not even dating, okay? We're just friends."

Jenna winked. "Whatever you say."

Gael sighed.

They *were* just friends, though maybe they wouldn't be much longer. November was less than a week away, which was great, because he really liked Cara. She was cool and pretty and in college, and yet somehow she still thought *he* was cool enough to spend time with.

She was the perfect girl.

She was just what he needed.

"Well, we're happy for you, Gael," Jenna said genuinely.

And he was happy, too.

Totally happy.

Pharrell-level happy.

And their pseudo-date at the movies was going to be great.

what would wes anderson do?

THE MOVIE WAS GOOD. REALLY GOOD. LIKE *RUSHMORE* and *The Grand Budapest Hotel* kind of good.

And the date or nondate or whatever it was—well, that was good, too.

Even though Gael and Cara hadn't seen each other or spoken much since Sunday, suddenly it felt like all was back on track, like on Monday maybe Cara really had just had a last-minute group project, like maybe she did want to give it a shot with him come November.

In the theater, as the playful music and too-bright colors had splashed across the screen, things had felt anything but friendly. Call him crazy, but Gael could have sworn that Cara had come on to him.

A few pieces of evidence supported his hypothesis:

First, when he'd picked her up at her dorm, she'd leaned right across the seats and kissed him on the cheek. It wasn't the kind of thing you just did to anyone. She wasn't French. Or even fake French, like Sammy.

Second, unlike at the tiny Varsity Theater, the seats in the theater in nearby Durham were the kind that had the armrest that you could flip up for ultimate make-out access (which he and Anika had done more than once). The arm had been up when they had sat down, but Cara made no move whatsoever to put it back. What's more, when Gael reached for it, she stopped him, claiming having it down would be too cramped.

Third, in the concession line, she'd suggested they share a large Cherry Coke. Sure, this was economically sound, but it had emotional meaning, too, no? Certainly it did. Gael would never think of sharing a Coke with Mason. The only person he ever shared with had been Anika—and Piper, of course, but she was his sister.

Finally, once the film started, and with each passing minute, Cara had scooted a little bit closer. At the beginning, she was all coy, legs pointed away, chin resting on her hand. But as the film progressed, as the symmetrical, shadow-box sets rolled into drawn-out tracking shots and iconic patterns, Cara kept inching closer and closer. First it was the way her knees were pointed. Then her Birks followed, landing just inches from his Chucks. Then, and he wasn't even sure how she did it because it's not like she was getting up and moving around or anything, but all of a sudden, her thigh was brushing his. They were both wearing jeans, so maybe she didn't notice.

But then again, maybe she did.

Their arms still weren't touching, and yet they too seemed to be moving closer together, like they had minds of their own.

A chase scene ensued, and Gael wondered how it would go if this were a movie about his life. Where would it begin? With Anika dumping him? Or with him meeting Cara?

Cara, his fun-loving, adorable costar.

Cara, with whom he'd shared a perfect movie Meet Cute.

Christ, he was starting to think in rom-com terms because of Sammy.

He tried to focus. If this were a Wes Anderson movie, how would it go?

Certainly, Wes wouldn't have him pass up a vivacious, beautiful girl who stole hot sauce and liked to hike and was just generally awesome? Just because he was a little less than 100 percent sure she was the one for him? That was silly.

Who said you had to be 100 percent, anyway? He'd felt that way with Anika, and look how that had turned out. Wasn't romance about taking a little leap?

(Sure it is. There are leaps of faith. Leaps into the great unknown. But you are certainly not supposed to "leap" when you're just not that into the person you're leaping for.)

Gael leaned a little closer, let their elbows just barely touch.

And yet, he couldn't help but think of what Sammy would say—Wes Anderson, *so formulaic*. He couldn't help but see her eye roll, that way she had of putting her hands on her hips when she wanted to make a point.

And that's why he was glad he was here with Cara, he decided.

He turned to her, caught a hint of a smile.

She may not be a movie buff, but on the upside, she definitely wouldn't tear it apart.

WHAT WOULD WES DO?

red light, green light

GAEL COULDN'T STOP TALKING ABOUT THE MOVIE THE entire drive back to Chapel Hill.

"Seriously, though, it was amazing," he raved. "What did you think? As good as James Cameron?"

"Well, nothing's as good as James Cameron."

He laughed, but he cringed a little inside because he knew she was at least partially serious. "Okay, but really?"

"Honestly?" she asked.

He nodded. "Honestly."

"It was kind of weird," she said.

"Well, yeah," he said. "Wes is kind of weird. But did you like it?" He swore that she looked like she was enjoying it a little bit, at least, in the theater.

Cara shrugged. "I mean, I liked being there with you."

Gael took a quick breath. "You didn't like *anything* about it?"

Cara bit her lip, thinking it over. "The girl had cool clothes, I guess."

Gael took a left onto Franklin and decided to try a new tactic. "So what did you dislike about it?"

Cara's eyes flitted out the window, and she fooled with the vents, flipping them back and forth. "It was just weird, like I said."

"That's all?" he asked.

Cara stopped messing with the vents and whipped her head around. "Yeah. And can we talk about something else, please?"

Gael nodded, trying not to be disappointed. He knew she wouldn't appreciate the movie like he would, he'd known she wouldn't dissect it like Sammy would, but he couldn't help wishing she had something more to say.

(I watched as Gael proceeded to do what any good Romantic would do: He ignored his disappointment. Cara, in turn, being the Serial Monogamist she was, tamped down her frustration.)

"Should we get something to eat?" he asked, changing the subject. "You like Spanky's?"

"I love Spanky's," Cara said.

At least they had that in common, Gael thought. His relief at the notion was a little too great.

✱　✳　✱　✳　✱

They parked behind Cosmic.

Gael checked his watch as they walked down the alleyway that bordered the dingy Mexican joint. Spanky's was closing soon.

"Hey, if they won't seat us this late," he said. "There's always nachos."

"Yes," Cara smiled. "We'll always have nachos."

He laughed. "You sound like Rick from *Casablanca*."

"Huh?" she asked.

"Never mind."

They crossed at the light, but a student on a bike breezed through the red. Instinctively, Gael reached out to stop Cara from walking forward.

(I cursed myself for not seeing the biker coming, for allowing them to have this sweet, movie-like moment.)

"You have to be careful," Gael said. "So many assholes on bikes."

"Thanks," Cara said, and then she cocked her head toward his. "You never know, some crazy girl might even hit you as she swerves away from a cute animal."

Gael laughed. "You don't do anything the normal way, do you?"

"Don't I?" Cara slowed her gait, looked up at him.

He shook his head no. "It's not a very regular way to make friends, running them down in the road."

"No," she said. "I guess it's not." She didn't drop his gaze.

But he did, before anything else could happen, because it was October still.

"Come on, let's see if Spanky's will take us," he said.

The restaurant was fairly empty. A few couples looked like they were finishing up their meals, plus a few people were at the bar, girls in their Friday-night heels and frat boys in polos that barely covered their beer bellies.

"Are you still seating people?" Gael asked the hostess.

"We sure are," the girl said with a bit of a forced smile. "Come on."

She seated them at the corner window, overlooking Franklin.

Gael shut the menu immediately. "No need to look," he said. "This is my favorite restaurant."

"I know," Cara said matter-of-factly. "You told me the night I met you."

Gael smiled. Maybe it hadn't all been him, that first night, he thought. Maybe even before he'd kissed her, she'd felt something, too.

"You sure know how to make a guy feel special, Cara Thompson."

And the words were ridiculous—she laughed and so did he. But the sentiment, at least, was real.

*   *   *   *   *

The upstairs corner table of Spanky's was Gael's favorite for a reason. A mass of windows looked out on the street below, peppered with students bustling—and occasionally stumbling—by. The upstairs was also perfectly in line with the swinging stoplights at the intersection of Franklin and Columbia, something Gael always loved to watch.

"Isn't it crazy how *huge* traffic lights are when you see them up close?" Gael asked.

(I gave her a little nudge. Reminded her that in past relationships she hadn't felt comfortable disagreeing with her boyfriend.)

Cara stopped eating and dabbed at her mouth with a napkin. "They don't really look all that big to me."

Gael sighed. They did look big and he loved how it made him feel small. He had the tiniest thought: *What would Sammy have said?* He quickly pushed it away.

"You have a little something right here." He motioned to the corner of his mouth.

Cara dabbed again with her napkin.

"Other side."

She tried again.

"Lower."

She pushed it at him. "Here, you do it."

Out of the corner of his eye, Gael saw the light turn green, and he leaned across the table and dabbed at the bit of sauce just to the left of her bottom lip.

(Their dinner was quickly turning into a full-fledged rom-com. I had to stop it.)

The light turned red, and he handed her the napkin again, leaning back in his chair.

Gael had ordered a steak sandwich, but despite his insistence that it was the best thing on the menu, Cara had chosen a pasta that she was picking at slowly.

"You don't like it?"

She shrugged. "It's a little bland."

(I *may* have tricked the chef into forgetting all the seasoning. Small victories, amirite?)

"I told you to get the steak sandwich," Gael muttered under his breath.

"What?" Cara asked.

"Never mind," he said.

Gael looked again at the traffic light and tried to gather his thoughts. If this were a movie (not a Wes Anderson movie, Gael thought, because Wes would find the whole idea very trite, but instead one of the movies that Sammy would probably like), the big giant traffic light staring them in the face as they ate their dinner would be a metaphor for their relationship. Like the game you used to play when you were a kid. Green light, go. Red light, stop.

He had to stop thinking about the whole world as if it were a movie.

The light turned green again, and his eyes drifted back to Cara, who was slurping sweet tea like her life depended on it, probably because she didn't like her pasta. In some ways, she was perfect. So what if she didn't like good movies? So what if she didn't understand that there was one thing and one thing only you should order at Spanky's? So what if she had a serious lack of childlike wonder when it came to traffic lights, which was especially strange for someone who regularly wore tie-dye shirts? Did it really matter?

And yet Gael couldn't help but think about what Sammy had said, about both of them being fresh out of relationships, about jumping in too fast.

The light turned yellow, and Gael overheard the conversation of the two girls at the next table, one of them going on about a roommate of hers who "can never be alone" and "just latches herself onto the first guy she stumbles across," which was particularly apt because Cara had lit-erally stumbled across him. He marveled at the irony that "Fools Rush In" was playing from the speakers.

Gael was scared of being hurt again, stepping out into the great unknown that was romance. He was scared of being wrong.

He wondered what would happen if he started dating Cara, how it would end. If he would be hurt again.

The light turned red.

(I gave him a bit of a nudge, pushed him onto the edge of a decision.)

"So do you still talk to your ex at all?" he asked.

The question caught Cara off guard. She choked a little on her sweet tea, but then instantly cleared her throat, composing herself.

"No," she said. "Why?"

"I was just wondering," Gael said. "I mean, it wasn't that long ago, right?"

Cara shook her head. "It was a couple of weeks before I met you."

"Do you still have feelings for him?" Gael asked. "How long were you together again?"

"Just four months," she said.

Gael had developed pretty intense feelings in less time than that. She seemed to sense his hesitation at her evasiveness.

"And to answer your question, no, I don't have feelings for him."

He nodded, but looked down at his mostly eaten sandwich.

"Hey," she said.

He popped a fry in his mouth and ate it quickly.

"Hey," she said again.

Gael looked up.

She didn't drop his gaze as she said the words. "You don't have to worry about him," she said.

And just like that, the light turned green.

cool hand fluke

AS GAEL AND CARA GRABBED THEIR COATS, GAEL HEARD an unmistakable voice.

"But it *says* you're open until ten. It says right there on the door."

Gael turned to see Anika, standing with Mason, just inside the restaurant door. The hostess's back was to them, but Gael could hear the edge in her voice. "We don't seat people past nine thirty, okay?"

Anika sighed loudly. "What if we promise to be fast?"

Gael had always thought Anika's gumption was amazing, but right then, it just seemed kind of rude.

(That's what happens when you people put your partners on pedestals. The fall is just that much greater.)

"Come on," Mason said. "Let's go somewhere that will take our money."

Cara turned to Gael and rolled her eyes, the kind of look that says, *Who does this girl think she is? Can she get out of the way so we can get out the door?*

Gael didn't even have time to take Cara aside and explain the situation because that's when Anika looked past the hostess and caught his eyes.

"Oh," she said, and Mason looked up then, too.

For a second, she and Mason just stood there, staring at him and Cara.

Without even thinking, Gael reached for Cara's hand and held it. Well, *grabbed* it.

Anika's face tightened, and Mason grinned.

"Look, I'm not going to seat you," the hostess said, wholly unaware of what was going on.

"Sure, got it," Anika said quickly, then walked out the door. Mason gave Gael a goofy wink before he made his exit.

Gael felt Cara tense up. He let her hand go.

He watched as the door closed behind Mason, and then they left the restaurant, too.

Luckily, by the time they got outside, Anika and Mason were well down the street, backs toward them.

Cara crossed her arms. "What in the world was that about?"

Gael bit at his lip and stole another glance toward Anika and Mason. They were far down Franklin, practically out of sight. Anika was walking pretty fast.

"Uh-uhm."

He turned back to Cara. "I'm sorry. That was my ex. I don't really have an excuse. I guess I just wanted to show her that I wasn't some pathetic guy who was still pining over her or something. I wanted to show her that I had found someone really cool."

(This is what I whispered in Cara's ear: *How dare he use you to make her jealous? Ditch him. He doesn't deserve you!*)

But it didn't work because Cara knew she'd done the same thing herself at the basketball game.

"Don't do it again," she said firmly. "Nothing happens until November, and if it does, it is *not* to make an ex jealous, okay?"

Gael nodded vigorously. "Okay."

Cara smiled.

(I internally cursed Cara's forgiving nature, even though it was one of the most wonderful things about her.)

"All right then, I should get back to my dorm. I'll walk from here." She held her hand up in protest. "Don't object."

"You sure?"

"I said, don't object," she said.

"Okay."

"But if you're down, do you want to do Halloween together? I've never been here for the big Franklin Street thing, and I hear it's awesome."

Gael hesitated. Halloween was the night before November. Was it possible that this would be their first real date?

But immediately he cursed himself for his hesitation. What in the world was he waiting for?

His face broke into an easy smile. "For sure."

familial advice: dad edition

GAEL GOT BACK TO HIS DAD'S APARTMENT JUST AFTER 10:00 that night.

"How was the movie?" his dad asked, practically pouncing on him as soon as he was inside.

Gael tossed his keys onto the counter. "It was good. Is Piper up?"

He shook his head. "She was tired after a big meal. I made pot roast."

Gael raised his eyebrows in mock appreciation. "Great," he said dismissively. "Sad I missed it."

He pushed past his dad in the tiny hallway and hung his jacket on one of the crappy dining chairs that looked like it came straight from a rando on Craigslist.

His dad followed him, not that there was much of a way *not* to follow him in such a tiny apartment. A history documentary was playing at low volume on the TV. "You know it's the second time you've missed Friday dinner," he said.

Gael turned to face him. "Is that a problem? You said it was fine last week."

His dad shrugged. "It's not a *problem*, per se, but is it going to be a new habit?"

"I don't know," Gael snapped. "I haven't worked out all my habits now that I have to live at two houses. *Sorry.*"

His dad walked up to the couch, grabbed the remote, and turned the TV off. "Is everything from now on *always* going to be a fight about me and your mom?" he asked.

"I don't know," Gael said. "Is it?" Gael knew he was being difficult, but he didn't exactly care.

(Before you get *too* frustrated with Gael, let me just tell you that, unless you've been through it personally, you have no idea how gut-wrenching divorce is. The heart feels like it would after a death, but the head can see that no one has died, that life is still going on—it's a unique grieving process, one that shouldn't be taken lightly. One that even I have trouble with sometimes, this situation being one of them . . .)

"Fine," his dad said. "But if you're going to skip out on dinner, can you at least tell me who you're hanging out with?"

Gael shrugged. "What does it matter to you?"

"A girl?" his dad teased.

Gael felt his face go hot.

"I knew it," his dad said with a smirk. He took a seat on the couch. "Are you worried you're moving a little quickly? You seem a bit nervous."

Gael mentally cursed his dad for being so damn touchy-feely and perceptive. Couldn't he be obsessed with sports and wings like other dads, instead of discussing emotions?

Mason's dad had taken him to Hooters for his sixteenth birthday. Gael's had bought him *The Art of Happiness* by the Dalai Lama and *What Color Is Your Parachute? For Teens.*

(In truth, Gael had always liked this about his dad. At Mason's birthday, he'd felt uncomfortable sitting in Hooters trying to focus on wings while Mason's dad ogled and flirted with every waitress. But it only made sense that Gael couldn't remember all that *right* at this moment.)

"I really don't need dating advice from *you*, of all people."

His dad looked taken aback by that—his head whipped back a little, his eyebrows scrunched up—but he paused, adjusted himself on the couch, took a deep breath, and didn't pursue it. "I'm just saying, you want to get to know a girl, and more than just how she looks in a dress, you know what I mean? When I met your mom, all I could think was how *smart* she was, how much she got me, how much she challenged me. Our philosophy professor even said we were two of his most passionate students—"

"I've heard this story a million times," Gael protested, his cheeks getting even hotter with anger. "Mom raised her hand to talk and you interrupted her. You got into an intellectually rigorous debate about your various philosophies, the professor goading you on. From that day forward, you started sitting next to each other in class. The rest is history. Blah blah blah."

He *had* heard the story a million times. But he'd felt little more than typical teen-son annoyance about it until now. Because as of a few months ago, *blah blah blah* no longer resulted in a happy ending.

His dad frowned. "I'm just offering advice."

Gael scoffed. He couldn't hold back his anger any longer. "Well, have you ever thought that maybe I don't want advice about you and *Mom?* We all know how well *that* turned out!"

Gael walked briskly to his room, which was only about four feet from the living room. He didn't even get to enjoy the luxury of slamming the door because he didn't want to wake Piper.

This apartment sucked, Gael thought bitterly. And his parents' breakup sucked, too.

And his dad going about like everything was fine? Well, that sucked most of all.

how gael's parents
actually met

JUST WANTED TO STEP IN AND CLARIFY A COUPLE OF things:

It doesn't much matter for the purposes of our story, but I think it's worth noting here that while the theme of his dad's advice was sound, not only was it a little awkward to bring up this story so soon after the split, but his version of the Arthur-meets-Angela story was, well, a little off the mark.

Replace your picture of a philosophy lecture hall with a seedy dive bar selling twenty-five-cent shots.

Angela was there with a girlfriend, who was interested in Arthur's roommate. After said roommate bought tequila shots for the group, Angela and Arthur did, indeed, realize they were in the same philosophy class, though they'd never even sat near each other before, much less exchanged ideas.

While their respective friends began to make out in front of the pool table, Arthur ordered two more tequila shots, and from there, the night kind of devolved . . .

At one point, Angela slipped off her stool and Arthur caught her. His act of chivalry didn't stop her from screaming, "*Of course* Nietzsche was a misogynist!" about three seconds later. And "if you think he's not, maybe *you're* a misogynist!" about three seconds after that.

She then challenged him to a game of pool, and she completely schooled him, even though she had to push her making-out friends out of the way each time she took a shot.

Inspired by her victory, Arthur ordered another round of celebratory shots. When Angela continued to go on about Kierkegaard, he climbed onto the barstool and shouted to anyone who would listen: "Soren Kierkegaard was the worst philosopher of all time!"

That's when the other patrons started to complain about the "lunatics screaming about Kierkegaard."

And that's when the bartender, not the professor, said, "You two are just about the most passionate philosophy students I've ever met. Now get the hell out."

And the rest is history, as Gael so exasperatedly put it.

Just wanted to set the record straight on that one.

scream queen

GAEL WOKE TO THE SOUND OF CRACKING EGGS AND the smell of frying bacon. Here goes another round at family bonding, he thought bitterly.

He hadn't slept well. He wanted to blame the hard mattress at his dad's place, which wasn't half as good as the one at home, but he also knew that at least part of it was due to the fight he'd had with his dad. But whose fault was that?

Gael got out of bed and threw on jeans and a T-shirt.

There was something else bothering him, too. Smaller, but important just the same. He'd texted Sammy last night, asking if she'd ended up seeing the Wes Anderson movie or not, eager to talk about it with her if she, for some reason, still had without him, but she hadn't responded.

He wondered if he'd offended her when he'd said no to the movie. He wondered if he'd somehow messed up their newfound friendship.

He wondered, ever so briefly, what it would be like if he and Sammy weren't friends. If they were actually something more . . .

Bacon crackled in the background and the smell accosted him. He pulled on his Chucks and tossed his phone into his pocket. He needed to get out of this stale apartment and get some air.

"Hey, sleepyhead!" his dad called as he walked past the kitchen.

"Where are you going?" Piper pouted. "Breakfast is almost ready."

"I need a walk," Gael mumbled. "Be back later. Don't wait for me."

Before they could protest, before he could fully take in the disappointed look on Piper's face or the concerned one on his dad's, Gael headed out the door and pulled it firmly shut behind him.

His dad's apartment complex was on the edge of Chapel Hill and Durham. Close to a big highway and a Walmart and a bunch of other stupid shit that he didn't really want any part in. It wasn't like his *real* home, where he could walk around, head to Franklin, even explore campus if he needed to get out of the house.

There was nowhere really to go but here.

Nevertheless, the crisp fall air felt good, and he headed down the concrete steps to the parking lot.

His eyes caught the COEXIST sticker on the bumper of his dad's hatchback.

Anika had once joked that it was always the assholes who had those stickers. He'd argued with her about that, defending his dad.

Now he wondered if she had been right.

He headed right, down the boring concrete sidewalk,

parking lot on one side, fake-looking grass and stones and stupid landscaping on another. Brick building after building stretched before him. They all looked the same. Still, he figured circling the complex a couple of times was better than sitting in the tiny apartment and waiting to snap.

He was about halfway around when his eyes caught a bright orange flyer taped to a lamppost.

SILVER SCREEN SCREAMS
An exploration of the horror genre—and Americans' deep affinity for it—from the 1920s until now.
Monday, October 29, 7 P.M.
Murphey Hall

Horror, he thought. Sammy's favorite. And at UNC, no less.

It was just the thing to make it up to her. She'd been a good friend to him over the last couple of weeks, and he didn't want to lose that, no matter what happened with Cara.

And the flyer, being all the way out here, so far from campus. It was strange, he thought. Almost like he was supposed to see it for one reason or another.

(Strange, indeed, Gael. Strange, indeed. *strokes imaginary goatee maniacally*)

Before he could stop himself, he took out his phone and called Sammy Sutton.

fifth period, third degree

ON MONDAY IN CHEMISTRY, MASON WAS AGAIN EARLY, but he didn't have an extra-credit project with him this time. He was sitting back in his chair, balancing on the back two legs, hands resting on the desk, beaming.

Mason leaned forward in his chair as soon as Gael threw his backpack down, the legs making a powerful *thunk*.

"So who was that?" Mason asked gleefully.

Gael felt himself blush. "What do you mean?"

"You know what I mean," Mason said.

Gael shrugged. "She's just a friend."

"Right," Mason said. "A friend who you go out to dinner with on Friday night and hold hands with."

Gael bit his lip and lowered his voice as more people shuffled into class. "I actually met her on my birthday after I left the restaurant, but she's just out of a relationship, too, and she thought we should just be friends until November."

"November's just around the corner," Mason said, moving his eyebrows up and down comically.

Gael took a deep breath. "I know."

"Well, I'm happy for you, dude. And Anika is, too, even if she was a little awkward." Mason's face looked a little hesitant, but Gael didn't ask why. It seemed safer to not talk about Anika right now. Well, not too much, at least.

"I gotta say, though," Mason said, just as their teacher, Mrs. Ellison, came in. "I don't know why, but I thought you and Sammy were going to end up together."

Gael blushed again.

And he felt his heart beat a tiny bit quicker at the prospect of seeing Sammy that night.

But Mrs. Ellison quickly began her lesson, so he didn't have time to ask Mason why he said it. All he could do was pretend to pay attention to chemistry and try not to get ahead of himself.

They were friends. That was it.

It was exactly what he wanted from her.

And even if it wasn't *exactly* what he wanted, he was pretty sure that that's what she wanted, at least.

it wouldn't be a good love story without at least one scene in the rain

ON MONDAY NIGHT, GAEL FOUND HIMSELF SITTING IN A hard chair in a dusty lecture hall, watching the ubiquitous vomit clip from *The Exorcist*, and pretending *not* to obsess about Mason's offhand statement (or potential truth-bomb?) while Sammy sat straight up in her chair so she didn't miss a thing.

The professor rambled on about absurdist horror and the heyday that was the seventies and early eighties as he cued up clips from *Re-Animator*, a psychedelic Japanese flick called *House*, and, of course, *Poltergeist* (which Gael had never found scary at all).

It all would have been very enlightening and thrilling if he hadn't spent most of the lecture trying to remind himself that, no matter what Mason had said, he was well on his way to dating *Cara*. Halloween was in two days. November 1 was in three. Now was not the time to be wondering about his romance potential with his little sister's *babysitter*.

Not to mention with someone who had become a good friend.

He'd lost his friendship with Anika to dating. He didn't want that to happen with Sammy, too.

The professor finished up with a clip from *Phantasm*, and then the lights flickered on and people shuffled out.

Sammy grabbed her backpack and slung it over her shoulder. She was wearing a vintage-y dress with polka dots, green tights, and a denim jacket. He couldn't help but think that she looked great.

"So awesome, right?" she asked. "I mean, the way he connected seventies horror to German Expressionism? It seemed so obvious once he said it, but I never thought of it that way before. Totally makes me want to rewatch all those slasher films."

Quite frankly, none of it sounded very obvious to Gael, but it didn't matter. He liked the way she got so excited about nerdy things.

"Very cool," he said, as he followed her out of the lecture hall and into the crisp fall evening. The lamplight cast an eerie glow over the UNC lower quad, and he zipped his jacket up all the way to block the wind. It was one of those fall days that feels like winter, that reminded you of what was to come.

Gael wondered where his life would be by the time winter arrived. Would he and Cara be properly in a relationship by then? Would they be sharing nachos and hunting for non-"weird" movies to potentially enjoy together?

A Christian campus group had set up a stand and was handing out hot chocolate, and Sammy ran ahead and grabbed two cups without even needing to ask if Gael wanted some. (I may have urged the organizer to plop her table right outside Murphey Hall.) When she came back, her cheeks were strawberry red and the lidless cups were steaming.

"For you, good sir," she said, giving a mock curtsy.

"Thanks." Gael nodded up the path. "Which way are you going?"

Sammy glanced back behind them. "I should probably get back to my dorm, but I'll walk as far as Franklin with you. I love campus at night."

So the two of them followed the brick pathway of the lower quad, walking slowly while they waited for the hot chocolate to cool.

"So what's your favorite horror movie?" she asked.

"Easy," Gael said. "*The Birds.*" Not even its recent association with Anika could quell his love for the masterpiece.

"Umm, *The Birds* totally doesn't count as horror."

"Of course it does!" Gael ventured a sip of his hot chocolate, but it was still too hot. "What are you talking about?"

"No one even dies," Sammy protested. "You can't have a horror movie without at least one death."

"The schoolteacher dies," Gael said.

Sammy rolled her eyes. "Fine, fine. Favorite *slasher* film, then. You know, where there's a killer, and the killer is not, like, a pigeon."

It was actually mainly crows and seagulls in *The Birds*, but Gael let that one slide. "*Psycho.*"

Sammy burst out laughing. "You, my friend, are a broken record when it comes to Hitchcock. You need to expand your repertoire."

They crossed Cameron Avenue and made their way onto the upper quad. It was quieter there, fewer people, less revelry. Just them and the moon. Gael shrugged. "He's the best."

"Right," Sammy said. "So then we should only read, I don't know, *War and Peace* over and over instead of other good books because they're not *the best book of all time*."

She had a point, he had to admit.

"Have you even seen *Friday the 13th*?" Sammy asked.

"That's the one with Freddy Krueger, right?"

Sammy stopped so short that a bit of hot chocolate sloshed out of her cup. "Wow, for a movie-lover you are totally lacking in the horror department. *Friday the 13th* is Jason. Freddy Krueger is—"

"*Halloween*," he guessed.

"No!" she said with disdain. "*A Nightmare on Elm Street!* And coincidentally Johnny Depp's first movie, *if* you need a reason to watch it besides the fact that it's fabulous. Michael Myers is *Halloween*. You *seriously* need an education."

And you're the perfect one to give it to me, he thought.

But then—*no*—that wouldn't really work. Once he and Cara were dating, he was certainly not going to be hanging out one-on-one with Sammy all the time. It would be, to borrow Cara's oft-used term, *weird*.

Sammy started walking again and took a sip of her drink.

"All right," Gael said. "I'm not so knowledgeable in what you would call true horror, you know, movies with no plot and a bunch of gore that aren't half as awesome as the shower scene in *Psycho*."

They reached the top of the upper quad. Franklin Street waited for them, with all its shops and restaurants and promise.

Sammy turned to him and smiled. "At least you stick to your principles," she said.

"Hitchcock forevah." Gael held up four fingers with his free hand.

They both laughed.

On Franklin, a group of sexy cops and nurses stumbled down the street, likely headed for a pre-Halloween frat party.

"So what are you doing for Halloween?" she asked.

Gael shrugged. "Nothing much. Just going to walk Franklin Street with Cara."

Sammy's eyes looked blank for a second, but then she smiled. "You guys are getting serious, huh?"

"I'm not sure about that," he said with a shrug. "But we're getting to know each other, I guess."

Suddenly, he had an idea.

(All right, all right, I may have given him said idea.)

"Did you want to come with us? I mean, since you're friends with her, too?"

(For a moment, Sammy considered it. I reminded her that she didn't have any set plans for Halloween, that her roommate had kind of been annoying her of late, and it would be more fun to go with Gael, anyway. I even let the streetlights catch Gael's eyes so they'd glisten in a way I knew she'd find downright adorable. But, alas, it was no use. Sammy was a Cynic, as I have mentioned previously. And she had too much freaking pride.)

"I have plans," she said, shaking her head. "And I also don't want to crash your date."

Gael was about to tell her that it wasn't a date—not officially, at least—but that's when it started to rain. *Hard.*

(Okay, the rain was my handiwork. This is a love story, after all. You might call it clichéd, but I call it classic.)

"Shit," Sammy said, as the two of them ran for cover under the nearest tree.

It began to rain harder.

Gael looked at Sammy, at her dew-kissed hair and the raindrops on her nose and her glasses, which were already fogging up. And all he wanted was to pause this moment, freeze it in place, just like this.

Their eyes met, and he could swear she was thinking the same thing.

Her lips parted ever so slightly, and he felt so nervous, like something might happen, something that could change *everything.*

But then she pressed her lips together and crossed her arms.

"I should go," Sammy said.

"You don't want to wait it out?" he asked. "It's pouring."

She shook her head quickly, making it clearer than ever that even if he wanted more than friendship, she didn't.

And without another word, she took off into a run down the brick sidewalk.

To Gael's surprise, the rain stopped almost as soon as she was gone. And so he crossed Franklin and headed toward Henderson Street, trying not to be too disappointed by her sudden departure.

He took another sip of his hot chocolate, but it had already gone cold.

gael's netflix queue, pre- and post-sammy

Pre:

2001: A Space Odyssey

Alfred Hitchcock Presents

Reservoir Dogs

Moonrise Kingdom

Breaking Bad: Seasons 1–6

Post:

When Harry Met Sally

Friday the 13th

Silver Linings Playbook

A Nightmare on Elm Street

Lovestruck: The Evolutionary Reasons Behind Why We Fall

scenes from a
baltimore dorm room

MY WORK IS A BIT LIKE JUGGLING. AT ANY GIVEN TIME there are tons of people who need me. And I do my best to balance it all. But sometimes, I don't. Sometimes, I focus so very much on diverting someone away from the *wrong* person and over to the *right* person that I lose sight of, well, the bigger picture.

This was one of those times.

While Sammy was running away from both the rainstorm and her own confusing feelings, her ex, John, was kneeling on a dusty linoleum floor, rummaging around in the chaos that lived beneath his lofted bed in Wolman Hall at Johns Hopkins.

John had once thought that his parents paying a boatload for him to go to school here would equal at least a semi-nice dorm room, but that certainly wasn't the case—not that he and his roommate, Juan (yes, John and Juan and at Johns Hopkins, no less), had worked to make it any better.

His hand hit the edge of a Tupperware tub, and he pulled it out from under the bed. A range of gadgets that his mom and dad had thought would be useful lay inside in a spaghetti-like tangle of cords.

Juan shuffled into the room. "What are you looking for?" he asked.

"The panini maker," John said, tossing his two Kraft singles onto a plate on his bed so he could better dig through the cords.

"Oh shit, man," Juan said. "I just took it to Cayden's this afternoon and forgot to bring it back . . ."

But John stopped listening. Suddenly he didn't care about the panini maker.

There in the bin, peeking out from beneath the George Foreman grill, which still had its tags, was *The Elements of Style*.

John stared at the vacant-looking watercolor basset hound on the cover. *How in the* hell *had this gotten in here?* he wondered. He could've sworn he'd intentionally left it at home to make his decision to break up with Sammy a little easier.

He glanced up at Juan, who was still going on about the panini maker while opening a fresh bag of Cheetos.

"It's okay, dude," John said. "Forget it."

He fingered the book in his hands.

"You okay, man?" Juan asked. "You look freaked out all of a sudden."

John didn't answer. He just stared at the book.

In the chaos of packing up his room, his mom or brother must have tossed it in last-minute.

All that summer, John had had the unshakable feeling of wanting to break up with Sammy, as he watched fellow high school couples dissolve in preparation for fall orientation. But she had been steadfast. She had asked him just once, right after graduation, if he thought they would stay together. It was in the middle of fooling around, and he'd said yes without thinking about much more than the fact that he wanted to get her top off. She'd never asked him again, instead frequently enlightening him on the average cost of flights from Baltimore to Raleigh and how long it would take to drive, with and without traffic.

John broke up with her on Labor Day, just before the second week of school. The long weekend had been a frat-party bacchanalia. On Friday and Saturday, he'd dutifully told every hot girl who tried to flirt with him that he had a girlfriend in North Carolina.

But then on Sunday, when AC/DC rang through a crowded, beer-stale basement, and a cute brunette leaned her head in close to his, he didn't stop her.

He broke up with Sammy the next day. Told her that he needed to be independent, to figure out who he really was, all kinds of vague bullshit that he knew she'd see right through.

"You hooked up with someone else?" she'd asked, her voice rising in a way that signaled tears were on the way.

She'd hung up on him before he could hear her cry.

He hadn't gotten to the chance to tell her that the drunken make-outs were less exciting each time. He longed to call Sammy and tell her about the antics of his dinosaur of a world civ professor, with his nasally voice and his Grateful Dead T-shirts and the hilarious way he had of saying "Byzantium." He wanted to tell her that he often wondered whether he'd rushed too quickly to embrace the no-strings-attached spirit of college. What if he'd already had the perfect relationship and had stupidly pissed all over it?

Now, here it was, the book she'd given him just a couple of weeks before he'd broken her heart. His dad was pushing him to do premed, but he wanted to be a journalist, and so she'd bought him *The Elements of Style*, the writer's standby.

He flipped it open to the first page and read the inscription:

J-
Don't ever let anyone tell you you can't be what you
want to be. You got this.
xxoo
Sammy

John glanced up, and Juan was staring at him, hand shoved deep into the Cheetos bag.

"What?" John asked.

"You wanna order a pizza?"

"No," John said quickly, glancing back to the book.

Before he could stop himself, he grabbed his phone and headed to the balcony where both reception—and privacy—were better.

I watched in dread—it was too late for me to do anything. I could see how he was hoping she would give him a second chance.

And I had the most horrible hunch that she would.

boys do cry

"HOW DO I LOOK?" PIPER ASKED GAEL PROUDLY AS SHE and his mom came down the hallway and into the living room on Wednesday afternoon.

Halloween had finally arrived, and Gael and his dad were standing awkwardly in the living room. His mom was going to take Piper trick-or-treating, but his dad had insisted on coming over to see her costume and take some pictures, as if they were all a big happy family once again.

Piper, for her part, reveled in the attention. She was decked out in pasty white makeup, a silver-gray wig, and bright feathers in her hair. Her dress poofed out at the sides to ridiculous proportions, and she held a fan his dad had gotten on Sunday at a junk shop in Carrboro.

Gael took a picture with his phone. "Awesome sauce."

"Qu'ils mangent de la brioche!" Piper cried with bravado. "That means, let them eat cake."

"I guessed as much," Gael said.

"But it actually meant that she didn't care about poor people," she said. "Sammy told me."

Gael couldn't help but laugh.

His mom pulled out her phone. "Let me get one of everyone."

"We're not even dressed up," Gael said.

His mom waved his protest off with a flick of her hand. "Who cares? I just want all of you together."

Why? he wanted to ask. *Why pretend like things are all right when they so obviously aren't?*

But he didn't want to cause a scene. He couldn't ruin Piper's moment—he'd already done plenty of that lately.

Gael and his dad took their places on either side of Piper. His sister's dress was so big his mom had to turn the phone sideways to get them all in. Piper struck pose after pose, while his dad beamed. His mom even jumped in for a selfie with the four of them.

After myriad photos, Gael cleared his throat and grabbed his bag of Halloween costume supplies. "I really gotta go," Gael said, when his mom refused to put the phone down.

"All right, all right," she said, popping the phone into her pocket and bending down to adjust one of Piper's ruffles.

His mom stood up and crossed her arms like she did when she was worried for his safety. "Now be careful, and don't do anything stupid. No drinking. No drugs. No hassling the cops. I don't want to see you getting pepper-sprayed on the news. Cops these days." She rolled her eyes.

"*Mom.*"

"Fine, fine. Off you go."

He gave his mom and Piper a hug, but he didn't bother saying bye to his dad.

His dad followed Gael outside, anyway. Since the split, Gael swore his dad was like a needy fourth-grader, looking for friends.

His dad clicked the key to unlock his Subaru. "Let me give you a ride to Franklin."

A small group of trick-or-treaters approached a neighbor's house nearby, and Gael watched as a mini ghost tripped over his sheet.

"It's not far," Gael said, shaking his head. "I'll walk."

"Come on," his dad said. "I want to drive you."

"I'm not even going to Franklin. I'm going to my friend's on campus first."

"Even better. I have to pick up something at my office."

"I thought you wanted to see Piper," Gael argued.

"She won't go till dark. There's plenty of time. Come on." His dad opened the driver's side door and hopped in, without giving Gael much of a chance to protest any further.

His dad checked about five times to make sure no kids were behind him, as he always did, then he backed out of the driveway and pulled down the street, heading toward campus.

When they got closer to campus, traffic was bad, as Gael had expected. Many of the revelers were already out, and Franklin Street was partially blocked off.

"Where does your friend live?" he asked.

"Avery."

His dad knew the campus well—even the dorm areas,

as Gael had learned—and soon, they were in front of Cara's dorm. His dad pulled to the side of the road and idled.

"Err, thanks for the ride." Gael reached for the door.

"Wait," his dad said.

Gael sighed loudly. "What?"

"What is up with us lately, Gael?" his dad asked. "I feel like you're angry with me all the time, and I can't help feeling like there's something else going on?"

Gael's shoulders slumped and he twisted the bag in his hands. "Do we have to talk about this right now, on Halloween?"

His dad turned to face him. "Yes, Gael, we do. You've been avoiding me like the plague since your birthday. I know that the split has been rough on you—it's been rough on all of us—but I don't think—"

"Oh, I'm sure it's been *really* rough on you," Gael interjected.

His dad scrunched up his eyebrows as a gaggle of Super Mario characters walked past their car. "What do you mean by that?"

Gael's eyes caught the very dorm he'd seen his dad walk into just over a week ago. He was unable to hold it in any longer. "Look, I'm not an idiot, okay? You may have fooled Piper but you haven't fooled me."

"Gael," his dad said seriously. "What in the world do you think you're talking about?"

Gael looked away from the dorm and stared through the side window as a group of girls in fishnet tights walked by, along with someone carrying a huge cardboard box and a can of spray paint into the dorm. He rushed at the words, afraid he wouldn't be able to get them out if he took his time. "I know you cheated on Mom, okay?" Gael felt hot tears on his cheeks, but he couldn't bring himself to look at his dad, to see the confirmation he knew would be there.

(Only I could see the ache that Arthur Brennan felt, the pain that twisted at his insides as he fought it down, because he knew, in this moment, more than anything else, he needed to be there for his son. Romantic love is one thing, but the love between a parent and child—well, that is *always* worth fighting for.)

Gael felt a hand on his shoulder. "Gael," his dad said.

Gael tried to shrug him off, but his dad wouldn't move his hand. "Gael," he repeated calmly.

"What?" Gael finally turned to face him, wiping the tears from beneath his eyes.

And the look on his dad's face—well—it said *everything*.

"I would never cheat on your mother, Gael. I want you to know that."

Gael sniffled. "You're lying. I saw . . ."—he paused to catch his breath—"I saw everything."

His dad folded his hands in his lap. "What do you think you saw, Gael? Tell me. I'm here."

Gael took a deep breath. There was no turning back now. He pointed toward the dorm in question. "I saw you go with a girl into that dorm."

His dad sighed.

Gael seized on the moment. "You had an affair, right?" he asked, hoping against hope that he was wrong. "With her?"

But his dad just shook his head. "Gael, that's where the Young Socialists club meets. I'm the faculty advisor."

"But you said you had office hours that day." Gael wiped a bit of snot from beneath his nose. "Why did you say that?"

His dad shrugged. "That's what I say for everything. It's just simpler than going into all the details. Jesus, son, that girl is twenty. Do you really think that's the kind of person I am?"

His dad pulled a pack of tissues from the console and handed them to Gael, who took them gratefully. "But what about the toothbrush? I saw one that wasn't yours in your bathroom."

His dad laughed a sad laugh. "You know what a freak I am about dental hygiene. I bought it at Student Stores because I'd had Indian food for lunch a couple of weeks ago."

"But it was pink," Gael argued.

"Yeah." His dad shrugged. "And it was the cheapest one at Student Stores."

Gael wiped at his eyes again. He felt ridiculous, like a child, and yet he felt the tiniest blossom of relief. "But the phone calls. Why are you always going into your room?"

His dad looked up at the ceiling, then back at the steering wheel, and finally back at Gael. Perhaps Gael had hit on some secret. He could tell that this didn't have as simple an explanation. His heart beat, once again, with that familiar fear.

"I was talking to my therapist," his dad said finally. "And I didn't want you kids to see me crying." His dad's face turned red, but he didn't stop. "Look, Gael, your mom and I thought it would be best to keep specifics out of it, but I guess we should have known that your imagination would run wild." He sighed. "I'm counting on you not to tell her this, and I hate to even put you in this position, but it was really important to her that we protect you guys."

Gael nodded.

His dad looked down at his hands, then back at Gael. Gael was shocked to see that his eyes were watery, too. "Your mom wasn't happy, Gael. She needed a change. She still cares about me, of course, but for her, it's just not the same."

The words hit Gael like a ton of bricks. "Oh my god, did *she* cheat?" he spit out.

His dad shook his head vehemently. "No. Your mom wouldn't do that. But she made it clear that she needed to move on."

Gael's head was spinning. "But then why is *she* the one who's crying all the time?"

His dad shrugged. "Because it sucks for everyone," he said. "Even if she wanted it, it still sucks."

"Why didn't you try therapy?" Gael asked. "You're always going on about how therapy is good for *everyone* . . ."

"We did," his dad said. He sighed. "You might as well

know all of it now. Remember last year when Sammy stayed late on Wednesdays, and we both said we had later office hours scheduled? Well . . ."

(This was the part that got me because, last year, if I had been there, maybe I could have helped Gael's parents. I could have reminded Gael's mom of all the natural ebbs, pushed her to give it more of a shot. I could have urged Gael's dad to fight for her, instead of taking her words at face value. But I didn't. For years, I wasn't there for them when I should have been. I was too sure of their success, too happy with my work. I was in love with love, just like Gael. I made the mistake that so many have, of thinking, even if only subconsciously, that if it's good enough, it doesn't need work.)

"I hate Mom," Gael said.

"Please don't." His dad's voice shook.

(Arthur Brennan, a certified Loyalist,[6] would never stop loving his soon-to-be-ex-wife. And he wouldn't stop defending her, either.)

"She loves you. I love you. We love each other, in our way. I'm sorry you had to deal with any of this." His dad put his face in his hands, stifling a sob.

And Gael didn't know what to do, except to say, "I love you, too, Dad." And then Gael wiped his eyes one last time and he got out of the car.

---

6. Loyalist (pardon the term, I love revolutionary history): One whose greatest strength when it comes to love is his or her devotion; one who may not fall as fast as the Romantic, but who falls way more deeply when it happens. May result in clinging to the past, overlooking a partner's flaws, and, frankly, allowing oneself to be walked all over. May also result in a knack for forgiveness that gives one the space to heal and love again.

the real worst day
of gael's life

YOU'RE WELL FAMILIAR WITH THE SECOND-WORST DAY of Gael's life. And now it only seems fit to share the first, to give you a look into the absolute worst day, the day that would hold that place for him for years to come.

It was a Saturday last July. When Gael and his family should have been grilling or visiting the farmers' market or rowing in Jordan Lake or one of a million other things they used to do as a family.

Because they *had* always been a happy family. Even though Gael knew happy families were rare, he'd taken it for granted.

(And I don't have to tell you that I'd taken it for granted, too.)

Gael knew something was off when his mom and dad walked into the living room, and his mom switched off Piper's educational program before Piper had even used half of her allotted screen time for the day.

"Hey," Piper said, running up to the TV and flipping it back on. "I still have forty-five minutes."

His mom and dad exchanged a look, and then his dad walked up to the TV and turned it off himself. "You'll get your forty-five minutes, but right now, we need to have, err, a family meeting."

His parents sat on the couch, side by side, a united front. Piper stayed on the rug where she'd been watching TV. Gael scarfed the remaining leftovers from last night's Italian dinner and waited for his parents to get on with it. He figured his mom had planned some new chore schedule or his dad wanted to do more outdoor activities together.

He was wrong, of course.

And he hadn't enjoyed the taste of chicken parmigiana ever since.

His mom took a deep breath and folded her hands in her lap. He realized, suddenly, that her eyes were puffy and that this was probably not about chores.

She looked at his dad again. "There's no easy way to say this . . ." Her voice dropped off.

His dad cleared his throat and then folded his hands in his lap. "Your mom and I have decided to go our separate ways. I'm going to be moving out of the house into an apartment in Durham at the end of the month."

The news shook Gael, shocked him. It was like everything slowed down, froze. His eyes drifted to the wall of family photos behind his parents—good times, bad times, *their* times—the pictures seemed to mock them all.

And then his gaze drifted to Piper, whose face was scrunched up like it was when she was trying to decipher a bit of French.

There was silence for—a minute? A second? An hour? Gael could hardly tell.

Go our separate ways. What the hell does that even mean? he wondered.

Piper was the first to speak. Her face unscrunched and hurt washed across it. "You don't want to live with us anymore?"

His dad's voice cracked. "Believe me, baby, I do. But"—he looked to Gael's mom—"we think this will be best for everyone. We still love both of you more than anything, and we still care about each other, but it will be better this way."

His mom stared at her hands, then up at Gael. "Sometimes people just don't get along as well as they used to," she said weakly.

Gael had a deep urge to rip one of the pictures off the wall, smash it over his knee, send glass shards everywhere.

Piper began to cry, and Gael had to look away. It was too hard to watch. Her face was too shiny, too red, too raw. "I don't want you to live somewhere else," Piper yelled. "I want you to live here!"

His dad stared at Gael, and Gael stared right back.

Gael realized this was serious, that they weren't changing their minds, that this wasn't some insane joke. That suddenly he was occupying a foreign world, and everything—from the photos on the walls to the marks in the dining room charting his and Piper's growth to the small crack in the sliding glass door from where a pigeon had flown into the window—well, it all felt suddenly so alien. So . . . off.

Gael couldn't stand being in the room anymore. He jumped up from the couch, walked as quickly as he could to his room, closed his door, and fell, facedown, in the bed.

And as he felt the tears dampen his pillow, he knew, deep down, that something huge had broken.

That a part of him would never feel the same about love, about family—about any of it—again.

night of the loving dead

IT WAS GAEL'S FOURTH HALLOWEEN ON FRANKLIN STREET.

The street was packed, as it always was. Each year, students, professors, some high school kids like Gael, and people from colleges nearby descended on the stretch of Franklin that edged the campus. The city estimated about seventy thousand people came each year, making it one of the larger centers of Halloween revelry in the country.

As such, people took Halloween quite seriously in Chapel Hill, turning three or four blocks into a giant party packed with people wearing everything from mass-produced costumes of the Party City variety to elaborate group numbers that made you wonder just how much the UNC freshmen were actually studying for their midterms.

Gael had been no exception. At the end of September, just a week or so before Anika had dumped him, he'd bought a couples' costume for the two of them, Marc Antony and Cleopatra, but given the Mason-and-Anika situation, Gael thought it was too weird to use it with another girl. (Not to mention, Cara certainly wouldn't have seen the Elizabeth Taylor and Richard Burton film it was based on.) And so, a quick run to Target this afternoon had resulted in enough zombie makeup for a *Walking Dead* episode. It wasn't as elaborate as his usual setup—past costumes had included the dude from A Clockwork Orange (bowler hat, eye makeup, and all) and the Joker from The Dark Knight—but it would have to do.

He and Cara had gotten ready in Cara's dorm. Cara's roommate took shots while her boyfriend touched up her Bride of Frankenstein makeup. By the time they were finished getting dressed, the roommate was on her third shot (luckily, Cara only had one, so Gael didn't feel too bad about not joining in), and both Gael and Cara were oozing blood and gore, faces pale and eyes rimmed in black.

Bonus: With all the heavy-duty makeup, Gael didn't think Cara could even tell that he'd been crying.

So now they were on Franklin, perfecting their jilted zombie walk, while Gael, unbeknownst to Cara, tried to hold it together after the revelation about his parents. Lucky for him, the street offered plenty of distractions.

"Can we agree that mimes are creepier than zombies?" Cara asked, as the black-and-white troupe headed off in search of their next target.

"One hundred percent yes," Gael said as a swarm of yellow Minions ran past them.

"Come on." Cara linked her arm through his. "Let's go this way." There was a small break in the crowd, where a group of firefighters in high heels had just sauntered through.

She let go of his arm and turned to face him. "Having fun?"

He nodded forcefully, afraid she'd prod if he didn't sound convincing. He couldn't deal with any more serious discussions. Not now.

"I'm glad I'm here with you," Cara said, and Gael wondered if maybe she'd had two shots when he wasn't looking. It wasn't exactly like her to be effusive.

A guy in a Jason mask stumbled past them, and for a second, he wistfully thought of Sammy, wondering where she was.

Cara shivered and started to rub her arms.

(Don't do it, Gael. Do not do it.)

"You want my jacket?" Gael asked. She was wearing a long-sleeve white shirt that they'd stained with fake blood, but had left her jacket at the dorm, complaining that it didn't go with her overall costume.

She shook her head. "I'm fine." But her chin was shaking.

"Come on." He started to unzip it.

"Uh uh," she said. "Really, I'm fine."

"Well, come here, then." He put his arm around her, pulling her close to keep her warm.

It was nice. It helped to quiet all the crap running through his head. A gaggle of Angry Birds and evil piggies ran past them, and he realized, suddenly, that this was exactly what he'd wanted, just a couple of weeks ago. It was November tomorrow. He was free to pursue Cara now.

So why did he suddenly feel so hesitant?

Cara nuzzled closer to him. "Thanks," she said. "Looks like I'm totally unprepared."

"Looks like you are," he said, a bit robotically.

He nodded to Cosmic, down the street. "You want to go get some nachos?" he asked. "Try to warm up a bit?"

Cara looked up at him and smiled. "That sounds perfect," she said. "Just perfect."

Cosmic Cantina was packed by the time they got to the front of the line, and it smelled like stale booze.

"Want to try and wrangle us a table?" Gael asked. "I can order the nachos. You want anything else?"

"Extra guac, please." Cara smiled.

"You got it."

Gael placed his order and stepped to the side, surveying the premises. At least half the diners were properly drunk, and the other half were well on their way there.

After Gael watched no fewer than three arguments break out and two bros fall to the ground, a guy in an apron whose forehead was beaded with sweat finally brought out the nachos. Gael's eyes flitted around in search of hot sauce—the only bottle was being used by a Superman who could barely sit up straight. "You have any more hot sauce?" he asked.

"Only in the back," the guy said.

"Okay," Gael said. And when the guy didn't move, Gael asked: "Can you get it?"

The guy looked at the crowd, then back at Gael. "I'm slammed, man."

"Please?"

The guy rolled his eyes and headed to the back.

Gael opened the container and popped a chip into his mouth while he waited. He couldn't help but think of the last time he'd had nachos, right before he'd kissed Cara. What had he been thinking, throwing himself at her like that?

He wondered again where Sammy was, then forced himself to stop.

"Here, man. Enjoy it," the guy said sarcastically.

Gael smiled at the fresh bottle of hot sauce and threw an extra buck in the tip jar.

He grabbed the bottle and pushed his way to the back. "Sorry that took so long," he said, as Cara sat up straight and brushed off the table with a napkin. "I had to ask them to get a fresh hot sauce out of the back."

"Oh." She tilted her head to the side, but she didn't say anything, just looked at him. Finally: "You didn't have to do that."

Gael shrugged. "I know how you love your hot sauce. I didn't want to disappoint."

"Still," she said. "I could have survived without it."

Gael flipped the lid open and doused the chips with Valentina's. "You could have, but you shouldn't have to."

She broke into a smile, one that was contagious. He smiled, too.

She didn't touch the nachos, just looked at him. "You know," she said. "It's almost November. No real harm in . . . err . . . pretending it's already here."

Gael felt his heart beat faster, and he couldn't tell if he was just nervous or what. *Was it the shots?* he wondered. *Had she really had more than one after all? She was being so forward all of a sudden.*

(Homegirl didn't need alcohol to be forward. She was a Serial Monogamist. And her vow was almost up.)

"Uhh," he stalled.

"What?" she asked.

"Wouldn't you rather say you made it the whole month?" He forced a smile.

Cara shrugged, popped a chip in her mouth. "Honestly, I don't really care."

He thought of what Sammy had said. *A whole month without dating someone!*

Wasn't it just a tad ridiculous that she wasn't even committed to going the whole month?

"I don't want to be on your friends' shitlist," he stammered, trying to buy himself some time. "So how about we hang out on Friday?"

She narrowed her eyes at him, trying to deduce what he really meant. But Cara wasn't the type to let a little hesitation on someone's part hold her back. Serial Monogamists don't really roll that way.

"All right," she said. "It's a date."

love and frisbee golf

THE NEXT DAY AFTER SCHOOL, GAEL TOSSED HIS FRISBEE toward the wire mesh basket of the fourth hole with avid precision. Just east of campus, Gael and Mason's favorite Frisbee golf course was technically part of UNC, but no one had ever given them a hard time about being there.

Gael had managed to make it home from the Franklin Street Halloween celebration relatively unscathed (and without any more uncomfortable overtures from Cara). They'd finished up their nachos, walked back toward campus, and parted at the post office, Gael trying not to think *too much* about the last girl he'd parted ways with at that very spot.

When Gael got home, his mom had seemed a little miffed when he didn't want to tell her anything about his night—she always stayed up late watching scary movies on Halloween and was waiting eagerly when he got in the door. But he knew if he so much as looked at her too long, he might lose it. And he'd promised his dad he wouldn't tell.

With so much bouncing around in his head, he practically jumped at Mason's invitation to play Frisbee golf. And as much as he was still not fully over what Mason had done, he had to admit that doing something normal with Mason, especially after all the drama yesterday with his dad, felt pretty damn good.

The Frisbee clanked against the metal pole and fell to the ground. Close, but no cigar.

"The hole in one evades you, my friend," Mason said.

It was properly cold out today, and they both wore UNC sweatshirts they'd bought together at Student Stores the previous fall.

"Since when do you say 'evades'?" Gael asked, laughing.

Mason shrugged, then tossed his Frisbee without much focus. It landed a good twenty feet from the basket. Frisbee golf was the one thing that Gael had always excelled at over Mason. Last fall, they probably played twice a week, but Mason never could get his wrist to stay straight when he threw it. It was a nerdy sport to be good at, but it was fun.

This fall, of course, they hadn't played at all until now.

Gael traipsed across the grass, kicking and crunching the leaves in his wake, Mason at his heels. He grabbed his Frisbee from where it had landed right next to the goal and plunked it in the basket. "A hole in two," he said. "Also not terrible."

Mason proceeded to toss the Frisbee too short and too far, as he always did, inevitably losing count of his number of shots. Finally, he just grabbed it, walked it to the basket, and pushed it in forcefully.

"Everything okay?" Gael asked. It wasn't like Mason to care about Frisbee golf.

Mason shrugged. "Anika's being weird," he said.

Gael raised his eyebrows. "Think she might be hooking up with your best friend? Oh, wait. I'm right here."

I probably should have said former, Gael thought. But then again, maybe he shouldn't have.

Mason rolled his eyes. "Very funny." He grabbed his Frisbee out of the basket and began to twirl it in his hands. "I think she was pissed that I didn't follow her stupid plan to get us all back together at lunch."

Gael shifted his weight from foot to foot. He didn't quite know what to say, so he didn't say anything.

Mason didn't wait for a response. "She said I should have backed her up on that, that if we were going to actually date properly, we couldn't keep acting all ashamed all the time."

Gael burst out laughing. "Dude, you don't act ashamed all the time. Neither does she."

"That's because Anika's always trying to save face," Mason said. "But she feels bad. Really bad. She talks about it all the time."

Gael kicked at a few leaves on the ground. "What do you want me to say?"

"Just hear me out for a second," Mason said, tossing the Frisbee onto the ground. "We got into this stupid argument last night. She suddenly didn't want to go out for Halloween because she felt so guilty. She kept talking about some Cleopatra costume she'd planned to wear with you?"

Gael laughed softly. It made him feel better that she remembered, that she cared, even if only the tiniest bit.

"And the weird thing is, any other girl, when things got to that point, I would have just moved on. But even after arguing, when we finally got to Franklin, like, I didn't even *want* to look at any of the girls in skanky costumes. I didn't even care."

"Cause you only wanted to look at her, right?" Gael asked.

Mason nodded. "Yeah." He picked the Frisbee back up. "And I know it's shitty of me to bug you about this. I know how completely screwed up it was to do what we did. I mean, if you did that to me now, god, I don't know, I'd want to kill you."

"I'm pretty sure I *did* want to kill you," Gael offered.

Mason started twirling the Frisbee again. "But you're my best friend, still. And I don't know, you're the only one I want to talk to about stuff like this."

Gael retrieved his Frisbee from the basket and walked to the next hole, Mason in tow. He was at a crossroads, he knew. He could throw a fit, explain to Mason that it was totally unacceptable for him to ask advice from him about his girlfriend after stealing said girlfriend.

Or . . .

Or Gael could recognize that what he and Anika had was maybe a lot more fantasy than reality. He could give credence to the fact that the sheer speed with which he was able to rebound showed she certainly wasn't the love of his life.

He could let himself see that Mason was, hands down, no holds barred, falling in love with Anika.

"Dude," he said, and he stopped walking. "Maybe you just like her a lot?"

Mason stopped, too. "Yeah, but what do I *do* about it? What if she freaks out and bails?"

Gael shrugged. "Maybe she will."

He could tell from the look on Mason's face that that's not what he wanted to hear. "And I'm supposed to just be okay with that?"

"Well, what else are you gonna do? Dump her so she doesn't dump you first?"

Mason laughed. "Sometimes it's tempting, honestly . . ."

(Defensive dumping is a staple of the Drifter playbook, I'll have you know.)

They reached the next hole, and Gael tossed the Frisbee toward it. It went way too far.

"I'm sorry," Mason said suddenly. "I'm sorry for being the worst friend ever."

"You're not the worst friend ever," Gael replied.

Mason shrugged. "I kind of am, though."

"Fine," Gael said. "You kind of are. But you're *my* worst friend. So I guess I'll just have to deal with it."

Mason freaking *beamed* at that.

Gael felt a weight lift, one he hadn't even realized was there until it was gone. It felt good.

"Well, since we're friends again . . ." Gael hesitated,

taking a deep breath. "I guess I can go ahead and tell you I found out yesterday that my mom was the one who wanted the divorce. Apparently, she just got tired of my dad or something. I'd thought for a while that maybe my dad had cheated, but that wasn't it at all."

Mason dropped the Frisbee. "Dude. You let me go on about Anika freaking out about Halloween, and you were holding on to this. That sucks, man. I'm so sorry."

Gael shrugged. "I don't know whether to be furious with my mom or just completely disillusioned with love in all forms."

Mason picked up his Frisbee and tossed it badly.

"It's better to have loved and lost than never to have loved at all, dude." He paused. "I saw that on Reddit."

Gael laughed out loud. "Is it, though?" he asked finally. "I thought it was. But now I'm not really sure."

Gael thought about Sammy, about how horrible it would be to lose her as a friend.

Mason nodded. "I think it is."

And for once in his life, Mason tossed the Frisbee straight into the hole.

"Hole in one!" Gael screamed. "Holy shit. Look at you, hustler!"

And as he jumped up and down and high-fived his friend, he had another kind of thought.

Maybe he didn't hesitate last night because Cara wasn't perfect.

Maybe he hesitated because Cara wasn't Sammy.

What if, this whole time, he'd been going after the *wrong* freshman from UNC?

baltimore bound

WHEN GAEL GOT BACK TO HIS HOUSE THAT AFTERNOON, he was feeling more like himself than he had in a long, long time. The relief of finally forgiving Mason was enormous. He even told his friend that maybe he and Anika could join them at lunch again soon—not just yet, of course, but eventually.

And, okay, add to the happy feelings a sense of resolve. Gael couldn't deny it any longer. He had feelings for Sammy, and he had to know if she did, too, before he could think seriously about dating Cara. It was only fair.

He wasn't sure exactly what he would say to her, but as he walked down the hallway and into the dining room, he was feeling especially light on his feet.

Sammy and Piper were at the table as usual. Piper was copying out French definitions, so absorbed that she barely even gave him a nod.

Sammy, on the other hand, looked up immediately and smiled. She adjusted her glasses. Gael had a sudden urge to take them off and kiss her like they did in the movies. He forced himself to focus.

"So, do I get all the juicy details?" she asked.

"Huh?"

"Your date," she said.

That got Piper looking up. "Date?" she asked.

He'd been so focused on what was on his mind that, for a second, he had no idea what Sammy was talking about. He stared blankly at both of them.

"With Cara?" she offered. "Halloween?"

"Oh," he stammered. "Err, it wasn't really a date."

Sammy shrugged, made air quotes. "Your 'hangout' with your soon-to-be girlfriend, then."

Piper looked from Gael to Sammy and then back again. "Wait, I thought *you guys* liked each other."

Sammy's face turned beet red, and she looked less composed than he'd ever seen her. Gael felt his own face heating up.

"No," he said. "I mean, well, the thing is . . ."

"I'm your babysitter," Sammy offered practically. "I can't date your brother. Plus, another girl has already won his heart."

"But you guys went to the movies together," Piper said, matter-of-factly. "That's like, a *date*."

"All right, all right, Little Miss Matchmaker," Sammy said, closing Piper's French book. "Why don't you go on the computer and get a little extra Wikipedia time in? I won't tell your mom."

"You guys are trying to get rid of me, right?" Piper asked.

"Yes," Sammy said.

"You just have to ask, geez," Piper said, and headed upstairs as fast as she could.

Sammy leaned back in her chair. Gael sensed that this was his moment. He just had to somehow find the right words.

"Well, that was awkward," Sammy said, looking at him and laughing.

"Uhh," Gael stuttered. He took a seat next to her. He could feel himself starting to sweat.

Sammy stared at him, but he didn't say anything. Her embarrassed blush was already fading. She crossed her arms finally, breaking the spell. "I do want to hear more about your Halloween."

He shrugged. Halloween was literally the last thing he wanted to talk about right then. "It was good, I guess. We were zombies. Umm, how was yours?"

She leaned her elbows against the table, tilted her head toward him. "You okay?" she asked.

Gael nodded quickly, wondering why this was so damn hard?

"Well, my Halloween was whatever. I didn't end up going out at all, actually."

Through the window outside, Gael saw three kids tossing a ball back and forth. He wondered, briefly, what Sammy had been like as a kid. Probably exactly the same. He scooted his chair back a little. He wondered how in the world to turn a boring conversation about Halloween into what he wanted to say—but what did he want to say?

"How come?" he asked finally. "I thought you said you had plans."

Sammy sat up straight and wrung the bottom of her T-shirt in her hands. "Yeah, I was supposed to do something with my roommate, but, well, I ended up just talking to John."

Gael felt his heart beat faster. He was taken aback completely. It was the last thing he'd expected to hear. "Your ex?"

She nodded. "He called me on Monday night . . ." Her voice dropped off.

"And what did he want?" Gael demanded.

Sammy hesitated. "He apologized for everything."

"Everything including *cheating on you?*" Gael asked.

"*Hey*," she said, raising her eyebrows. "He explained everything. He got with another girl at a party and then broke up with me the next day. I'd hardly call it cheating."

"Oh, that's convenient," Gael said. He could feel himself getting worked up, his face becoming hotter.

"Well, it's true," she argued. "He said he was just scared by the idea of a long-distance relationship. Since Monday, he's been texting a bunch, and he even sent me flowers on Tuesday. It was so sweet."

Gael took a deep breath and tried to gather his thoughts.

Sammy fiddled with Piper's French book, avoiding his eyes. "Anyway, I'm going to Baltimore tomorrow night. I figure I need to see him in person to figure out if we can give this a real shot again."

"What?" Gael asked, dumbfounded. "You're actually thinking about taking him back?"

She turned to look at him, narrowing her eyes. He noticed a tiny tear in the page she'd been messing with. "If Anika had come back apologizing, don't tell me you wouldn't have given her another chance. And John didn't, like, start dating my best friend behind my back. He made out with one girl at one party, one time. It's college."

Gael opened his mouth but found he had nothing to say. Finally, he shrugged. "Whatever. It's your life."

"You know, you're not being very supportive. We're supposed to be friends," she argued.

And it was only as she said it that he realized how desperately he wanted *not* to be friends with her.

But it was too late. That was painfully clear.

"I should get some homework done," Gael said quickly, standing up. "Safe travels."

He didn't wait for her to say anything else, just headed back to his room.

text therapy

GAEL STAYED IN HIS ROOM THE REST OF THE AFTERNOON. He put on *Rushmore*, a movie Sammy did *not* like, and texted Mason furiously with the new developments.

so i actually thought i liked Sammy but she
just told me she's getting back with her ex

> what happened to hippie chick?

i don't know i can't stop thinking about Sammy

> i knew it! so why are you NOT stopping
> her from getting back with douche-face?

because it's her life, and that's what she wants

> LAME

she's not into me, it was clear from our convo

> i always thought she was, tho

if she was why is she getting back with douche-face
nice name, btw

>   don't know, dude, don't know.
>   girls r weird
>   anika is freaking out bc i assumed we
>   had plans tomorrow without asking

LOL don't ever assume with Anika
little bit of advice for ya

>   go talk to Sammy
>   NOW!!!!!

i can't 😞

>   what are you going to say to
>   hippie chick? aren't you supposed to
>   be like her boyfriend very soon

dunno 😞

>   damn, ur more of a player than me

😞😞😞

familial advice: mom edition

GAEL DIDN'T GO OUT AND TALK TO SAMMY, DESPITE Mason's persistence. In fact, he was still in his room when his mom got home just past five. After a minute, she knocked on his door.

He sat up. "Yeah?"

"Can I come in?" she asked.

He sighed. "Sure."

She walked into the room, glanced at the movie, which was almost done, but she must have figured he wasn't *that* into it because she smiled and leaned against his closet. Her eyes weren't puffy today. *Good for you*, Gael thought bitterly.

"I never got to hear about your Halloween," she said, as she absentmindedly folded a T-shirt that was thrown across his computer chair.

"It was fine," he said with a dismissive shrug.

She set the T-shirt down and crossed her arms. "You're awfully quiet. And you were last night, too. Is something wrong?"

Gael stared at her. He wanted, so badly, to yell. To tell her that, yes, sometimes it felt like everything was wrong, like their whole family was ruined, that he could never really have faith in love again. He wanted to tell her, finally and honestly, just how much the divorce was breaking his heart. He wanted to ask why in the world she'd decided to leave his dad.

But he couldn't. He'd made a promise.

She smiled mischievously. "So Dad tells me you were meeting some mysterious stranger who goes to UNC. Is she nice? What does she study? I want to hear all about her."

"I don't really want to talk about it," he said.

And he didn't. But especially not with her.

"Oh, come on," she said. "You gave me all the fun details when you were first dating Anika."

It was true, he had. Because she'd seemed so sad and broken up from the split, and because the two of them had always been pretty close, and because it seemed like in that first month, all he could do to try and make her happy was to talk to her constantly, to tell her every little bit about his life, to be her distraction.

He'd felt so bad for his mom. But now he knew the split was all her doing.

"I don't really want to talk about dating with you, Mom," he said.

She threw her hands in the air and smiled sheepishly. "I know, I know, I'm your boring old mom."

But he shook his head. He sat up in the bed, grabbed the remote, and paused the movie.

He took a deep breath.

"I know that you're the one who ended things with Dad," he said finally.

Her jaw dropped. "How did you—"

"Dad told me. It's not his fault," he rushed to add. "I forced his hand. I thought he was cheating and he had no choice but to tell me the truth."

She put her hand to her mouth, then dropped it again. "Oh, Gael," she said. "Oh, sweetheart, I'm so so sorry."

"Don't," he said bitterly.

"Just let me explain—"

"I don't want to hear anything you have to say," he said. "Dad already said enough." And he rolled over to face the wall until he heard the door close and his mom's steps down the hall.

scenes from a chapel hill high school hallway

THE NEXT MORNING, GAEL WALKED BRISKLY THROUGH the high school parking lot and toward the building's double doors. He wanted to catch Mason at least a few minutes before class started. He was eager to tell him about confronting his mom, and he didn't really think emoticons would do the convo justice. But Gael was later than usual, which meant that he had only a couple of minutes at most to talk to Mason, and the thought of waiting until chemistry seemed unbearable.

The halls were already swelling with students. In the main hallway, Danny caught his eye and waved, but Gael just gave him a quick nod and kept walking. Mason knew his parents better than anyone else from his friend group. Gael was hoping Mason would find a way to somehow make it all okay.

But as he pushed through clacking lockers and giggling freshmen, getting closer to Mason's locker, Gael saw Anika standing with Mason down the hall. Gael stopped short, causing a brawny football player to run into him, cursing.

"Sorry, dude," Gael said over his shoulder and then trained his eyes on his friends.

Anika's hands were balled up at her sides. "That's not what I meant!"

Mason stood stock-still, looking utterly and completely lost. "But why else wouldn't you want to hang tonight? We had it all planned out. I even got reservations."

Gael remembered what Mason had texted last night. Was Anika really that mad that Mason had assumed they'd hang out that night? Sure, she was independent, but it seemed ridiculous, even for her.

"I just said I changed my mind, okay? I'm allowed to change my mind."

"I know, but I don't see why," Mason pleaded.

Anika shook her head and stepped back. "You know, maybe this isn't working, okay?" And she flipped around and stomped straight toward where Gael stood frozen, watching it all play out.

Anika stopped suddenly when she saw him. "How much of that did you hear?"

People pushed around them, but it didn't seem to matter if anyone overheard. It felt for a second like it was just the two of them, like it used to be sometimes. "The important parts, I think," Gael said.

Anika shrugged. "Well, now you know that I'm a bad person all around," she said. "Have a good one."

"Wait," he said. This wasn't right. He'd seen the way she was with Mason. That's what had made Gael and Anika's breakup so hard.

Anika stopped. "I don't need another lecture, Gael." Her

eyes flitted around the hallway. "And in front of everyone again. I really don't."

A few passersby stole looks at them. She was right, the rumor mill would be busy today. But Gael didn't want to lecture her. That was the last thing on his mind. "Did you guys really just break up?"

Anika sighed, and he could see that her eyes were beginning to water. "I don't know," she said.

"What happened?" Gael asked. "Mason really cares about you. I'm sure there's an explanation for anything he did—"

"He didn't do anything," Anika said. "Besides give me the time of day even though you were his best friend."

Gael scrunched up his eyebrows. "You're telling me you're mad at him, even though you're the one who, technically speaking, cheated?"

Anika's arms dropped to the sides. "It's messed up. I know. But . . . well—" She fooled around in her backpack and pulled out a book. She pushed it into Gael's hands.

Relationship Karma:
What Goes Around Really Does Come Back Around

Gael took the book from her. It looked like something his dad would read. In fact, it looked like one of the books his dad had already given him.

"What's this?" he asked.

"It's just a book I found on Amazon, okay? I ordered

it after your birthday dinner. I don't know, I was feeling a little bit bad about being a complete and utter harlot, all right?"

Gael shook his head. "You're not a harlot. Geez. And who says *harlot?*"

"Anyway." She took the book back and stuffed it in her bag, looking around to see if anyone had read the bright words of the new age title. "It basically says that anything that starts in chaos ends in chaos. And that it's not good to rack up such bad vibes in relationships. It will affect your relationship karma for the rest of your life—and maybe your lives after."

Gael laughed. "You needed a book to tell you not to cheat on your boyfriend?"

She crossed her arms. "You know, forget it. I'm sorry I told you." She started to turn away.

But Gael reached for her shoulder. And instead of shaking him off, Anika turned to face him again.

His hand dropped back to his side. It was the moment of truth, the chance to detail out just how shitty she had treated him, but not in an explosive, hysterical way like he had at his birthday dinner. This time, it would make an impact, he could tell. This time she was actually listening.

And yet . . . he had a feeling she already knew how much she'd screwed up.

He had a feeling he should maybe worry about his own relationship karma.

"Look," he said. "You really hurt me, and that's not going to just disappear."

Her mouth fell to a frown. Gael held his hand up. He wanted to finish what he had to say. She looked down at her feet as he spoke: "But I did put a lot of pressure on you by saying 'I love you' so fast. And you definitely handled it in a completely shitty way, but I don't know, maybe it's how it was supposed to happen. Maybe you wouldn't have done something so crazy if there hadn't been good reason for it."

Anika didn't say anything, just stared at the dusty tiles beneath her feet. She was wearing the red Mary Janes again. He'd always love those Mary Janes, even if he didn't love her anymore.

"Just don't ruin a good thing with Mason on account of me," Gael said finally. "Life's too short not to be with the person you want to be with."

The warning bell rang, and Gael walked away without another word, feeling strangely, insanely *good*.

let's not even pretend to work on the chem lab, shall we?

GAEL FOUND THAT HE WAS NERVOUS AS HE APPROACHED chem after lunch that afternoon. He hadn't spotted Mason or Anika at lunch, and he worried that, despite his motivational speech, Anika still hadn't been able to forgive Mason—or, more accurately, forgive herself.

But when Mason walked in, his fears were instantly dispelled. There was a conspicuous smudge of lip gloss on the bottom of Mason's mouth.

Gael rolled his eyes. They hadn't been arguing at lunch. They'd been making out. Typical Mason. And Anika, for that matter.

Mason sat down, beaming.

"Dude," Gael said. "I realize you've been known to wear makeup on occasion, but there's really no need now. I'm no longer being tortured by assholes in middle school."

"Huh?" Mason asked.

Gael pointed at the bottom of Mason's lip.

"Ohhhhh," he said. He laughed. "You caught me. Is that weird?"

Gael nodded. "Yeah, but it's okay."

They both laughed.

It was lab day in chem, and Gael and Mason spent the whole of the period doing just about nothing with their microscope.

Instead, they talked about Gael's mom—Mason urged him to listen to whatever she had to say, but Gael didn't want to. He already knew enough.

And the reservations Mason had made for dinner with Anika that night were at 411 West, the pinnacle of the Chapel Hill dating scene. Gael chuckled to himself imagining gangly Mason sitting in front of a white tablecloth and trying to choose the right fork.

And finally, they talked about Cara.

"So you're supposed to see her this afternoon?" Mason asked. "And it's like, *the* afternoon?"

Mrs. Ellison walked past them, and for a second, Gael pretended to adjust his microscope.

"Yeah," he said. "I didn't know how to cancel. And I don't know if I should."

Mason raised an eyebrow. "You're sure Sammy doesn't like you?" he asked.

Was he? Gael wondered.

(And it made me so sad because I knew deep down that he shouldn't be sure, that he still had a shot, but I also know that while Romantics fall hard, they take rejection even harder, especially at the beginning.)

Gael was sure of one thing—that Sammy had been right. Timing *was* everything. Maybe if things had happened sooner. Maybe if he hadn't been distracted by Cara.

But how was he supposed to compete with her high school sweetheart? Sammy loved John. That was so clear from all the times she'd talked about him before he'd broken up with her. How could Gael ever compete with that?

(Romantics love deeply—beautifully—but their fatal flaw is doubting deep down whether anyone can truly feel as strongly about them.)

"I don't think it's going to happen with Sammy," Gael said finally.

Mason scrawled gibberish on their worksheet, pretending to do something as Mrs. Ellison looked over. After a minute, he shrugged.

"Cara's cool. You do like her. So what if she's not *the one?* Maybe she's the one for right now?"

the pros and cons of dating gael, according to sammy's scratched-out list

PROS:

- ~~NICE EYES~~
- ~~AT LEAST HE'S 18~~
- ~~FELLOW MOVIE LOVER~~
- ~~SEEMS LIKE HE TREATED ANIKA REALLY WELL BEFORE SHE SCREWED HIM OVER~~
- ~~WE COULD CARRY ON A CONVERSATION ABOUT ALMOST ANYTHING~~
- GOOD OLDER BROTHER + FAMILY LOVES ME
- ~~ACTS LIKE HE LIKES ME, LIKE HE LIKES ME ALOT~~
- HE'S GAEL

CONS:

- IN HIGH SCHOOL
- 18 IS STILL WAY TOO YOUNG
- OBSESSED WITH WES ANDERSON EVEN THOUGH HIS MOVIES AREN'T EVEN THAT GOOD
- A MOVIE LOVER SHOULD REALLY HAVE WATCHED AT LEAST ONE SLASHER FILM WITHOUT PROMPTING
- ~~IS THE OLDER BROTHER OF THE GIRL I'M BABYSITTING~~
- IF HE HAD REALLY CARED ABOUT ANIKA, WOULD HE HAVE REBOUNDED SO QUICKLY?
- TALKS TOO MUCH
- ~~TOO NICE~~
- HIS EYES AREN'T REALLY THAT AMAZING
- IF HE REALLY LIKED ME, HE WOULDN'T BE THROWING HIMSELF AT CARA

the kiss: part one

THE AFTERNOON ROLLED AROUND, AND NO MATTER how nervous Gael was about it, it was time to see Cara. Her self-imposed month of singlehood was officially over, and he'd decided to take Mason's advice. Why not? Cara made him happy, for the most part. Could you really ask for more than that?

It was an unseasonably warm day for November, and Cara had suggested a picnic on the lower quad.

As he walked across campus, students were tossing Frisbees and drinking out of cups that probably held way more than coffee, taking advantage of one of the last pleasant days of fall.

(Fun fact: No fewer than five future couples would meet on the quad that Friday. There was something about impending winter that made people pair off like their lives depended on it.)

Gael spotted Cara spread out in front of Wilson Library. She was sitting on a red blanket and was even wearing a polka-dot dress.

"Wow," he said, as he walked up and sat down next to her. "You look great."

"Don't act so surprised," she laughed.

"You know that's not what I mean."

She produced a pair of bagel sandwiches and pushed a warm paper cup into his hand. "I got us lattes from the Daily Grind," she said cheerfully. "It's not as good as Starbucks, if you ask me, but I remember you saying it was your favorite."

"You didn't have to go to all this trouble," he said.

"It wasn't trouble at all," she said. "Here, have a sandwich."

Gael took his gratefully and ate, eager for something to do. They chatted a bit, about the weather, about the coffee, about how the kids next to them were so bad at throwing Frisbees.

Eventually, the sandwiches were gone, and the lattes were finished, and there was nothing left to distract them anymore.

Cara scooted closer to Gael on the blanket, and he hesitated, but then he wrapped his arm around her shoulders. She leaned closer, the empty cup still in her hands, then she began to pick apart the cup in pieces, while Gael's hand gently stroked her shoulder. He was unsure of where to go from there.

Finally, when the cup was disintegrated, Cara looked up at him, and he looked down at her, and they both leaned in, and their lips touched for the second time.

one-track mind

FRANKLY, I WAS JUST A TEENSY BIT WORRIED ABOUT THE kiss. But when I took a little glance into Gael's mind to see if I still even had a shot at making this work, here, readers, is what I saw:

SAMMY SAMMY SAMMY SAMMY SAMMY SAMMY SAMMY . . .

And before you start feeling sorry for our dear Serial Monogamist friend, here's what Cara was thinking:

I'm sure I'll like the next kiss better.

I'm sure we'll grow to be really excited about each other.

I'm sure, at least, that I'll have someone to hang out with these next few weeks . . .

Bingo! It looked like my plan wasn't *that far* off track after all.

the kiss: part two

GAEL WAS KISSING CARA WHEN HE HEARD POUNDING feet coming at them.

He didn't even have time to figure out what was going on before a giant Frisbee player backed right into him, tripping over him and wrenching him and Cara apart.

"Holy shit!" Gael yelled. "What the hell?"

The guy quickly rolled back up, grabbed his Frisbee. "Sorry dude. Didn't see you there."

(All I had to do was send the Frisbee that much farther than it was supposed to go. Sometimes, I swear, my job is almost easier than it should be.)

"Ass!" Gael called as the guy ran off.

He turned to Cara. "Are you okay?"

She nodded slowly, looking more shocked than anything. And then, suddenly, she looked like she'd figured something out, solved a problem, realized something big.

(Me again! I'd bought both of them just enough time to reflect, to step out of the kiss, to see it for what it really was.)

"I need to get back to my dorm and study," Cara said. She stood up and began to pack everything into her bag.

Gael didn't even try and stop her. Instead, he stood up,

helping her gather her stuff together. He understood her meaning exactly.

"Go," he said kindly. "I've got stuff to do, too."

And with that, my friends, Gael's untimely Rebound officially came to an end.

to catch a thief

ONCE CARA HAD ALL HER STUFF PACKED AND THEY'D exchanged an awkward good-bye, Gael rushed out of the lower quad, past Student Stores, and toward South Campus as fast as his legs would take him. With any luck, Sammy hadn't left for the airport yet. Maybe he still had a chance with her, he thought hopefully—maybe he could *make* the timing be right!

He ran fast, dodging students carrying books, a big guy with a trombone, and a tiny girl with a ridiculous amount of photography equipment strapped to her back.

But he stopped once he got to the bell tower. There was one huge problem. He had no idea where Sammy lived. Sure, he was heading toward a lot of dorms, but she could live practically anywhere.

He tried calling her, but the call went straight to voice mail.

He looked down at his watch. It was almost 5:00. Had she told him when her flight was? He couldn't remember that, either, but he didn't think so.

He paced back and forth in front of the bell tower, trying to rack his brain for the name of her dorm. He vaguely remembered her saying it once when they were walking to the horror movie lecture.

Hines something? It started with an H and had two words, he was almost totally positive. She'd made some joke about it being like the Howard Johnson motel.

Even if he could remember the name of it, he had no idea where it was.

He needed a map.

Filled with resolve, Gael turned around and sprinted to Student Stores, which he could only hope would have a good map.

His foot caught on a "brick monster," as Sammy called them, one of the uneven bricks in the sidewalk, but he caught himself before he fell and kept on running.

He took the steps two at a time to get to Student Stores. Once inside, he pushed through the rows of UNC sweatshirts and other paraphernalia to the book area. Laminated fold-up maps were sitting in a bin, right next to the blue books students used to take exams. He flipped one over: $3.99.

Gael glanced over to the register. A mom, likely in town for a football game, was arguing with the cashier about the discount level on a sweatshirt.

Screw it, he thought.

He did a quick perimeter check and shoved the map into his pocket, then walked, as casually as he could manage, toward the back door.

"Hey," a voice said behind him.

The hair on his neck stood up.

"Hey, I saw that."

Gael looked back quickly to see a short, compact dude staring back at him. The guy looked like he could *run*.

Without thinking about the consequences, without considering the fact that it would almost certainly be easier to just call it a misunderstanding and pay for the damn map, without thinking—well—at all, Gael grabbed a tower of XL UNC sweatshirts and flung it to the ground. People burst into yells all around him as a blanket of school spirit covered the ground.

Then he ran, faster than he'd ever run before, weaving in and out of confused students and horrified parents until the double doors were in sight and he was out, out into the fall air, taking the steps three at a time, holding up his hand to stop campus traffic, and dodging back behind the bell tower.

Gael's heart was racing, his clothes were soaked with sweat, and he could barely breathe. He wrestled out of his sweatshirt and tried to find his breath.

Then he peeked around the side of the tower and gazed toward Student Stores. The guy who saw him was nowhere in sight. Nor were campus cops or irate store managers or SWAT teams.

He'd made it. He had never, ever stolen something before. He had never even considered it, much less engaged in a high-speed foot chase. It felt good, exhilarating. This was the new Gael Brennan! A maniac for romance!

The bell tower chimed five times. It was now 5:00.

Not wanting to lose any more time, he unfolded the map as quickly as he could and scanned it for H-names. Horton, Hardin, Howell—there was nothing with two names. His eyes continued to search while students walked past, talking animatedly, excited for the weekend.

Finally, at the very bottom, about as far away as possible—Hinton James.

That had to be hers. He was sure of it.

Now if he could only make it there in time.

the hitchhiker's guide to unc

BETWEEN THE SWEATSHIRT IN ONE HAND, THE MAP IN the other, and the backpack on his back, Gael found it hard to maintain a run as he rushed to South Campus, easily a twenty-five-minute walk away. He went south on Stadium Drive and couldn't help but slow down a bit to catch his breath. If he kept this up, by the time he got to Sammy's, he wouldn't even have the stamina to make the speech he hadn't had a chance to prepare.

"Coming through," Gael heard someone say behind him, and he turned to see a dude on a golf cart, trucking down the brick pathway, right toward him.

Gael froze as a thought filled his mind. A nutty thought. But he'd already stolen a map, knocked over a tower of sweatshirts, and made a successful escape. What was one more ridiculous move in the quest to get to Sammy in time?

Gael held his hands out in front of him, the universal symbol for stop.

"Whoa there," the driver said, slowing down.

Gael rushed up to the side of the cart, hand on the frame so the guy couldn't get away without a chat. "Where are you going?" he asked.

The guy was wearing a blue track jacket and a hat that said UNC ATHLETICS. His face was creased with laugh lines. "The Dean Dome. Is there an emergency, son?"

"The Dean Dome is right next to Hinton James, right?" he asked.

The guy adjusted his cap, nodded. "Do you need me to call campus police? Has something happened?"

Gael shook his head vehemently. "Listen, it's not an emergency, but, well, it kind of is. I'm okay, don't worry, I just need to get to Hinton James, like, *right now.*"

The guy paused, looked Gael up and down, then adjusted his hat again. "Well, hop in, then."

Gael hit him with a string of fervent thank-yous and climbed in the passenger seat.

The man took off, the UNC landscape flying by at what seemed like record speed. Gael had never stolen anything. And he had never hitchhiked. Sure, it wasn't actual hitchhiking, the highway kind, but he still felt pretty damn good about himself. It wasn't everyone who could manage to hitch a ride to South Campus without, well, a hitch.

They turned down another path, leaving Kenan Stadium behind them. "So." The guy smiled. "Who is she?"

"Huh?" Gael asked.

"Or he," he added. "I guess these days I really shouldn't assume."

"No," Gael said. "She. Well, you shouldn't assume, yeah, but she is a she. But how did you know, though?"

He laughed, as the rising brick structures of the South

Campus dorms appeared before them. "It's after five on a Friday and you're headed down to the dorms. I'm willing to bet this so-called emergency isn't that you didn't get your philosophy paper in on time."

Gael smiled. "Well, she's awesome. I'll say that much."

The man stopped at the corner of Manning and Skipper Bowles Drive. "I'll have to let you out here. The dorm is just down the path."

"Thanks," Gael said, grabbing his backpack.

The man winked. "That's what I'm here for. Go get her."

the girl next dorm

IT WAS ONLY AFTER THE GOLF CART PULLED AWAY THAT Gael realized there were *two* paths. *Two* dorms in this vicinity. He pulled out the map, but in his agitated state, he could barely tell left from right, much less north from south.

Shit, he thought.

Gael took a guess and headed to the right, running as fast as he could manage down the path. As he approached the front door, Gael stopped a dude in a hoodie who looked mildly friendly.

"Is this Hinton James?" he asked.

"This is Craige, man."

Double shit.

"It's the next dorm," the guy said, but Gael didn't even stop to thank him. He just turned and bolted.

In minutes, he was in front of Hinton James. By the grace of God, Sammy had once mentioned that she lived on the top floor, so Gael knew that, at least.

By the double grace of God, students were regularly coming in and out of the front doors, so he didn't have to worry about not having a key to get in.

He breezed in the double doors and headed straight for

the elevator bank in the middle. He pushed the up arrow about fifteen times.

"Chill, dude. It'll come." A tall skinny girl in workout clothes gave him a bit of side-eye.

He ignored her attitude and took a risk. "You don't know Sammy Sutton, do you?"

She raised an eyebrow in obvious annoyance and took a long swig out of her Nalgene bottle. Finally: "You do know that there are like a thousand people who live in this dorm, right?"

Triple shit.

The elevator came, and he avoided the eyes of snippy miss yoga pants as he walked in, pressing the button for the tenth floor.

The climb up was miserable—the damn elevator seemed to stop on every floor. Plus, everyone was so laid-back and relaxed, so happy for the weekend—chatting with friends, some already smelling of booze. *Just get off quickly and let me make my way,* he wanted to scream. *Big stuff on the line here!*

After what felt like hours, he arrived on the top floor. Gael was the only one left by this point. He bounced anxiously on his feet as the rusty elevator doors took forever to open.

Finally, he was out. The dorm was a mess of balconies, like a crappy motel. Gael didn't know quite where to start, so he made for the first door. Out in the fresh air again, seeing the campus from the top balcony, he headed to the right and into the first hallway. It had four doors. One of them was open. He gave it a knock as he poked his head in.

Mumford & Sons was playing on a computer, and a bunch of pasty guys were holding forties.

"Sorry, but do you know Sammy Sutton?" he asked, without much hope.

"Pay the entry fee, and we'll give you an answer," one of the guys said.

"Huh?" Gael asked.

"One shot, sir," the same guy said.

Gael shook his head. "It'll make me sick, and . . ."

The guy's friend shrugged. "No can do, then."

"Are you freaking kidding me?" Gael asked. "Can't you just point me to her room?"

The third guy stood up, opened the fridge. "All right, dude. Come in. If not a shot of alcohol, a shot of pickle juice will have to do."

The guy didn't wait for Gael to answer, just took an economy-size jar of pickles out of the fridge and deftly poured a shot like he'd done this a time or two before.

He handed the shot to Gael. "Everyone must pay the entry fee."

Gael took a deep breath. It smelled disgusting. But he tilted it back anyway.

It accosted his senses, making his lips pucker. If only Sammy knew the lengths he was willing to go to find her.

"Happy?" Gael handed the shot glass back as a pickle-y burp snuck up on him.

The guys clapped.

"Now can you tell me where she lives?"

"Sorry, dude, don't know her."

"You're shitting me," Gael snapped. And he rushed out of the room before he did something stupid like punch someone when all of the guys were probably stronger than him.

Gael headed into the next suite of rooms. There was an open door, and a different girl sat on almost every available surface. There had to be eight of them packed in, at least.

"Hey," one of them said. "A dude!"

"Do you guys know—"

But the girl didn't let him finish. "Okay, I'm glad you're here because we really need a guy's opinion."

"Jessica!" another girl yelled.

But Jessica just shooed off her concerns with a wave of a hand. "Okay. So Madison met a guy at a party last night who's also in her history class, and he friended her on Facebook, but he sent her this message that said"—she grabbed Madison's phone for utmost accuracy—"and I quote, 'Do you know what the history reading is?'"

The girls all stared at Gael.

"Yeah," he said. "So?"

Jessica rolled her eyes. "So the debate is, is it date-y or not date-y? I say date-y, because I know for a fact that his roommate, who I talked to last night, is in the class, too. So why wouldn't he just ask *him* for the reading?"

Madison sighed. "But we talked about so many more

interesting things last night. And I told him I was probably going to see the Breakfast Club, the eighties cover band, you know, at Sigma Chi tonight, and that leaves him a super-open window to ask me out. But instead, he's messaging me about history?"

Gael shrugged. "Maybe he's testing the waters."

Jessica burst into cheers, along with a few of the other girls. "Told ya so!" she said.

Even Madison was happy with his answer. "Maybe if you write back, then he'll mention the show," Gael added.

More cheers.

"Thank you, kind dude," Jessica said.

"Now I need your help." Gael crossed his arms. "Do you know Sammy Sutton?"

He watched in agony as all eight girls shook their heads. And then he bolted. He had no more time to waste.

The next few attempts were equally unsuccessful. He interrupted girls putting on makeup for a night out, guys arguing about whether or not to get extra cheese on their pizzas, a huge group crowded around a laptop watching YouTube videos.

Not one of them knew Sammy. He was about ready to give up.

Finally, Gael headed into a room at the end of the balcony. A guy was doing pull-ups on a bar installed in the doorway. "Do you know Sammy Sutton?" Gael asked as the guy's chin crested the metal bar. The guy immediately dropped down and wiped his hands on the towel at his waist.

"Yeah," he said. "She lives on this floor."

Thank God, Gael thought.

"Do you know where?" he asked.

"Through the door there, out the other door, head to the right, and it's the second or third suite of rooms, I'm not quite sure."

He must have noticed Gael's look of confusion and despair because the guy immediately started laughing. "Come on," he said. "I'll take you."

He led the way back down the hall and through the doors into the room with the elevators.

He turned to Gael as they passed through the door on the other side. "You're not some creepy stalker guy, are you?" he asked.

Gael shook his head. "Sammy and I are friends. I just forgot which room was hers."

"Got it." He walked to the right and then entered the second door to a hallway with another four rooms. He motioned to the first one.

"There it is," he said. "Not sure if she's home."

"Thanks, man," Gael said, and the guy headed back out.

Gael stared at the door. There were a bunch of silly photos and a large whiteboard tacked onto the door. The whiteboard read:

"Can you guess the movie quote? NO GOOGLING!"

Gael laughed. Of course, Sammy would use movie trivia to decorate.

And then his eyes locked on the quote just below:

Too many guys think I'm a concept, or I complete them, or I'm gonna make them alive. But I'm just a f&#@ed-up girl who's looking for my own peace of mind. Don't assign me yours.

Beneath the quote were a string of guesses in different handwriting.

Punch-Drunk Love

Lost in Translation

Silver Linings Playbook

But Gael knew that they were all wrong.

He also knew that Sammy was still thinking about him. She *must* be.

He popped open the marker hooked onto the board and wrote:

Eternal Sunshine of the Spotless Mind

And then he knocked on the door.

how to lose a girl
in ten minutes

GAEL HEARD SHUFFLING BEHIND THE DOOR, AND HIS stomach seemed to leap into his throat. If it was her, what was he was going to say? *Don't go! Ditch your ex-boyfriend! Be with me, instead!* All the words that came to his head sounded horribly cheesy and pathetic.

It didn't matter. It was too late to turn back. And he didn't want to, anyway.

Finally, the door opened.

His heart sunk. It wasn't Sammy.

"Can I help you?" a red-haired girl said. Gael figured she must be Sammy's roommate.

"Err, is Sammy here?"

"And you are?" she asked, leaning against the open door.

"I'm Gael? Her friend from—well—she babysits my—"

"Oh, I know who you are." The girl broke into a smile.

He felt himself blush. *This has to be a good sign, right?*

Her smile faded as quickly as it came. "Sammy's not here, though. She just left for the airport like ten minutes ago. You could try her phone? I think it was dead, though. She left here in kind of a rush."

293

He nodded. "Yeah, she didn't answer."

The girl shrugged. "Maybe try her again. She'll probably be able to charge it once she gets to the airport."

Gael stepped back, dejected. "Well, thanks, anyway."

"Good luck, Gael," she said. And she smiled again, then closed the door.

He stood there for another minute, unable to move.

Ten minutes. A lousy ten minutes in which he was shooting pickle juice and analyzing Facebook messages.

Sammy had told him timing was everything.

But he'd never known how right she was until this very moment.

familial advice: piper edition

GAEL WAS FEELING TOO DOWN ON HIMSELF TO EVEN think about walking home. He opted instead for the Chapel Hill bus. He tried calling Sammy two more times on his ride, even leaving her a ridiculously awkward voice mail where, like a total weirdo, he said, "I have something I want to talk to you about." But it was no use—her phone remained off.

By the time he got back to his house, he was feeling worse than ever. It was too late. She would fly back to Baltimore, John would seriously be upping his game to make up for cheating on her, and all the old feelings would come rushing back. Whatever he and Sammy had—or almost had—would become but a distant memory.

Gael's mom and Piper were in the dining room when he walked inside. They were making a Halloween slideshow on his mom's MacBook.

His mom smiled a weak smile, and Piper cheerfully said, "Hello," but he didn't have the energy to return the sentiment, so he walked past them without saying anything. He couldn't handle the thought of being around anyone.

Gael headed into his room, threw his backpack down, and locked the door. He popped *Eternal Sunshine* into the

Blu-ray player. It would probably make him depressed, but he wanted to be depressed.

His doorknob rattled.

"Go away," he said. "I don't feel well."

The doorknob rattled more. "Let me in!"

"Piper," he yelled. "Just leave me alone."

The doorknob stopped rattling, and he heard her steps padding down the hall. He started the movie.

But in less than a minute, the rattling was replaced with urgent banging.

Gael jumped out of bed and whipped the door open.

"Jesus Christ," he said. "What's your problem?"

Piper put a hand on her hip. "Mom says you're not supposed to say that. She says that even if we don't go to church, it's disrespectful to people who do."

Gael rolled his eyes. "Mom's not perfect. And neither am I. What do you want?"

"Mom wants to know if you're going to Dad's tonight and if you're going to drive me later."

"I don't know," Gael said. He started to close the door.

Piper pushed with all her might on the door. He gave up and let her in.

"You *can't* skip again. You skipped last week *and* the week before. It's not as fun without you."

"Fine," Gael said. "I'll drive you to Dad's, and we'll all have an *awesome* time. Can you just leave me alone right now, please?"

She sat down on the bed. "You look sad."

"I don't want to talk about it," Gael said, flopping back on the bed.

"That means you *are* sad," Piper said. "Because you didn't say you weren't."

"So?" he asked.

"So are you going to tell me why? I'm a good listener. Dad says."

And then maybe it was because Piper could be so damn sweet sometimes, or maybe it was just because he felt so crappy that he needed to tell someone, but he spilled it. All of it. His realization that he wanted to be with Sammy, the map thievery, the trip to her dorm, and last but not least his complete and utter failure at stopping her from heading off to reunite with her ex.

Piper's mouth was hanging open by the time Gael was done. But then, quick as can be, she shut it, crossed her arms, and tilted her head to the side.

"What?" he asked.

She flailed her arms about dramatically. "Why are you sitting here moping and not going to find her?"

Gael turned his palms up. "It was probably a sign. It's not supposed to be. It would have just gone to hell, anyway."

Piper huffed. "You're supposed to say *heck*."

"Well, it would probably have gone to *heck*, okay?"

Piper shook her head. "No, it wouldn't."

"Umm, have you seen Mom and Dad? Something terrible always ruins everything. Happy endings are just in Disney movies. I'll pass on all that unhappiness, thanks."

She crossed her arms. "Mom said she still loves Dad, it's just different now."

"Oh, did she?" Gael scoffed.

"Really, she did. I asked her if she was sad that she married Dad because now she cries a lot, and she said that she would do it all over still. She said that when you meet someone as cool as Dad, you have to go for it."

Gael shook his head. "No way that's what she said."

Piper nodded vigorously. "It is!"

He paused. "Really?"

"Uh huh."

Gael was quiet for a moment. On the one hand, his mom's words made him feel better. Even if they didn't make up for all the bad things these last few months, at least it didn't mean that everything had always been bad.

But on the other hand, this was doubly as scary.

You could love someone, you could pick the right person, you could give your life to them, and you could. Still. Get. Hurt.

His heart ached for his dad. And for his mom, for that matter.

And for himself and Piper and everyone.

Gael didn't want to get hurt again. And yet deep down, he knew somehow that all of this meant getting hurt. That all those big feelings only happened when you put your heart in someone else's hands. They could crush it, like Anika did. They could change their minds after twenty years, like his mom.

But maybe missing out was worse than getting hurt, Gael thought. *Maybe Mason was right—maybe it was better to love and lose than to remove yourself from the game completely.*

"Did Sammy tell you what airline she was on?" Gael asked.

"No," Piper said.

Gael sighed. Of course she hadn't. Why would she?

"But Mom would know," Piper added. "She drove her to the airport. She only just got back."

Gael jumped out of bed, quickly pulled his shoes on. "I love you, Piper," he said, as he made his way out the door.

"I know," she said matter-of-factly.

He should never have let her watch *Star Wars.*

rush hour

GAEL'S MOM PRACTICALLY FELL OUT OF HER CHAIR when she heard that he A.) liked Sammy and B.) was rushing to the airport in the name of a ridiculous, grand romantic gesture. Not only did she give him the flight info, but she sent Piper over to their neighbors and insisted on giving him a ride herself.

They didn't talk much, but his mom drove like a maniac, swerving around cars, pedal to the metal, pushing her smart car to the ultimate max.

It was 6:45 by the time they got to the Raleigh–Durham Airport.

There was a huge line of cars when they got to the RDU departures terminal.

"I'm going to run," Gael said. "Screw this."

His mom nodded, and he reached for the door.

"I love you, Gael," she said.

He looked back at her.

She took a deep breath. "And I want you to know that I love your dad and I love your sister. And I'm sorry for all the hurt that I've caused. I'm sorry for putting you through all this." Her voice choked, just a little, but then she quickly pulled it together. "It doesn't change how much I love you all, though. Please know that. It's just that sometimes people grow apart."

Gael shook his head. He didn't have time for this, and yet he desperately wanted to hear what she had to say. He was still holding out for a real reason why she'd left his dad.

"What does that even mean?" he asked.

She sighed. "You're going to go off to school next year. And it's going even faster with Piper. You're dad is content. This is all he wants. You guys and Chapel Hill and his work and all that."

"And what do you want?" Gael asked, his bottom lip beginning to tremble. "To move away and never see us again?"

She shook her head. "Of course not! Not for years, at least. But I don't know, down the road, maybe? Or maybe I'll travel. Maybe I'll take Piper to France for a summer. Maybe I'll quit teaching, do something else."

"But why couldn't all that happen with Dad?" he asked.

His mom looked down at her hands, then back up at him. "Because it's not what your dad wants. He needs someone who wants to stay put. I need someone who wants to keep going. And I thought for a long time that you guys would be enough, and I love you so much that I feel guilty even thinking it, but I have to live for me, too."

Gael stared at his mother. At the woman who'd been there for him every day since forever, the woman who'd done something so unexpected as this, the woman who, until now, had never really appeared to Gael like a separate person, with her own life and her own problems that didn't all revolve around being his mom.

(And even though she was talking to Gael, in a way, she was talking to me, too. Angela Brennan was a Dreamer[7] when it came to romance—she always had been—and maybe, as awful as it was, Arthur wasn't her dream anymore. Maybe even though what they had was beautiful, it wasn't meant to last forever. Maybe there really wasn't anything I could have done, even if I had been around more. Maybe this was how it was all supposed to work out.)

"I really should go, Mom," Gael said.

(All of a sudden I wanted so badly for him to forgive her. Because all of a sudden, I had forgiven her.)

She smiled. "I know. I just wanted to say that. I'll be waiting in the short-term parking. Take your time."

He hopped out of the car as quickly as he could, shutting the door behind him. She began to pull away.

(I gave him one last tiny nudge.)

---

7. Dreamer: One who views romance as the ultimate act of self-fulfillment, seeking constant challenge and growth. May result in a constant desire to define and improve the relationship, make plans for the future, and lose faith when the future doesn't turn out exactly as imagined. May also result in incredibly deep romantic connections and emotional bonds.

He started for the sliding doors, but then he turned back, rushed at his mom's car, knocked on the window.

She rolled it down. "Did you forget your phone, honey?"

Gael shook his head. "I just wanted to say that I love you, too, Mom."

r-d-eff you, part one

GAEL HURRIED THROUGH THE DOORS MARKED DELTA AT RDU's Terminal 2, his heart racing a million miles a minute.

Miraculously, there was no one in line. Perhaps the universe was actually looking out for him for once? he thought.

(The universe has always been looking out for you, Gael.)

He stepped up to the counter. The half-cocked plan he and his mom had formed on the way over was to buy a ticket for the same flight so he could get through security and hopefully still stop Sammy. He had about three hundred dollars in his checking account, and she'd even fronted him an extra hundred; he was praying that it was enough.

The woman behind the counter looked to be in her thirties, with layers and layers of makeup and eyebrows arched so she looked permanently perky. "How can I help you?"

"I'd like to buy a ticket for the seven-forty-five flight to Baltimore," he said, trying to sound at least somewhat calm.

"Cutting it a little close, aren't we?" Her plastered-on smile got wider.

Gael shrugged sheepishly.

"Let's see if we have any seats left."

Her fingers went to work on the keyboard, typing furiously, while her eyebrows moved up and down with almost every new click of the Return key.

Finally, she said, "You're in luck. We have one seat left. Is coach all right?"

Gael nodded. *Thank God.* He didn't even want to think about how much a first-class ticket would cost. "Coach is perfect."

"Great," she said. "The total with taxes and fees will be one thousand, two hundred, and six dollars and thirty-three cents."

Holy. Shit.

It took Gael a minute to find his voice. "That's coach? One way?"

She nodded, her smile getting just a tad less bright. She could see through him already, he was sure of it. "Would you like me to book that for you, sir?"

"That's the cheapest you have?" he asked. He'd assumed it would be a little expensive, last minute and all, but a thousand freaking bucks? *Jesus.*

"It's the last seat, sir."

He looked behind him. A line had formed in the few minutes he'd been there. People were beginning to look a tad impatient. So was the formerly perky ticket lady. "Would you like me to book that for you, sir?" she asked again.

He stalled. What the hell was he going to do now? "It's just that I'm sure my friend didn't pay that much. I just thought . . ." His voice trailed off.

And that's when her smile disappeared completely. She stared at him, lips pursed, like he was a misbehaving student in a kindergarten class. "This isn't Expedia, sir. We're not a discount service. We're an airline. And this is a last-minute purchase."

"I know, but—"

"Would you like the ticket or not, sir?"

Then Gael had a thought, a ray of hope. He didn't need to go to Baltimore. He just needed to get into the terminal.

The man behind him cleared his throat loudly.

"No," Gael said. "But is there any ticket I could buy that leaves tonight that's less money?"

The lady sighed. "What destination, sir?"

"It doesn't matter," he said.

"It doesn't matter?" She raised an eyebrow.

"No, see, I just need to talk to my friend, so I really just need a ticket to anywhere."

She lifted her hands from their resting position on the keyboard and crossed her arms in front of her chest. "*Anywhere* isn't exactly a destination I can plug into my system, sir."

"Can you believe this guy?" someone muttered behind Gael.

The counter lady just stared, waiting.

"Okay, Charlotte?" he asked.

Her hands went to work again. After another few minutes: "There's a nine o'clock flight to Charlotte." She smirked. "Let's get straight to the total cost, shall we? Eight hundred, ninety-two dollars and fifty-two cents."

Holy. Shitballs.

"D.C.?" Gael asked.

He looked behind him. The guy in the front of the line looked straight at him and said, "You're going to make us all miss our flights, you ass!"

She continued typing. Finally: "Nine hundred, thirty-four—"

"You know what, just forget it," Gael interrupted her.

And he walked away to the raucous applause of everyone else in line.

sammy sutton unplugged

SAMMY SAT IN A CHAIR NEAR GATE C7, ALMOST POSITIVE she'd forgotten something.

She'd packed in a rush, even though she'd made it to the airport in plenty of time. But between her hallmate bailing (that was my work, y'all) and having to hit up Mrs. Brennan for a ride, she was a little . . . flustered.

She unzipped her bag and checked it again. Toothbrush, check. Razor, check. Makeup, check. Cute underwear, check. Birth control, check.

She wondered if John had really only made out with that girl at the party before they broke up, or if he'd done more.

The thought hit her so hard it was impossible to ignore: Gael would never, ever, ever have cheated on her. He simply didn't have it in him. He wasn't that kind of guy.

She shook her head. This trip was not about entertaining a silly crush she had on a *high school student*. This trip was about trusting John. Restoring what they'd had. Getting it all back on track.

And yet, she was sure she'd forgotten something.

It didn't help that her phone wasn't charged and her

stupid charger had finally conked out after being finicky for weeks.

She guessed it didn't much matter, though. John would be there to pick her up for sure, and he would surely have an extra charger in Baltimore.

It's not like fooling around on the Internet would calm her nerves anyway.

So she opened up *Candide* and tried not to focus on the anxiety building in her chest.

r-d-eff you, part two

GAEL HAD DEVELOPED A NEW PLAN.

Sure, he couldn't afford a ticket, but perhaps he could still get through security. He had his ID. He didn't even have a bag. He'd pass through the metal detector without a hitch. He just had to convince someone to let him through.

It was 7:15. He didn't have much time, but he had to at least try.

He walked up to the security checkpoint like nothing in the world was wrong, as if he actually had his shit together and *belonged* inside the airport. He held up his ID. The lady took it. "Boarding pass?"

Gael tried his best to look young and naïve. "My dad had it, and he already went through. We got separated. I can get it on the other side."

She tilted her head down, nonplussed. "I can't let you through without a boarding pass, sir. You can get another copy at the airline's ticket counter."

He bit his lip. "It's just that I'm going to be late and I really need to just get through."

She shrugged. "Not my problem, sir. Please step aside."

Shit.

He tried a new tactic. "Okay," he said. "Look. I just

need to get through security to talk to someone. It's really important that I talk to her right now, before she gets on the plane. It's kind of like an emergency. And her phone is dead. So if you could just let me through—I'll go through the detectors and everything like I had a boarding pass, and obviously I'm not going to be able to get on a plane without one—then I can get hold of her and tell her what I need to tell her."

The woman laughed, stared at him, broke into a grin.

Whoa. Had his plan actually worked?

"Not a problem, sir. Just answer me one question, and I'll let you right through."

Hot damn, Gael thought. *Maybe things really had loosened up around here. Word on the street was you didn't even have to put your liquids in plastic baggies anymore. Who knew?*

"Sure," he said.

"Can you tell me my birthday, sir?"

"Your birthday?" he asked.

"Uh huh." She nodded.

"I don't get it. How would I know *your* birthday?" he asked.

She smiled even wider. "Well, sir, it seems that you're under the impression that I was born yesterday, so someone as smart as you should certainly be able to deduce my birthday."

Double shit.

"Next," she said.

He had no other option but to remove himself from the

line. He shook his head as he walked away. He'd been so stupid to think that any of this would work.

But then, in a flash, he saw his opening.

Literally. An opening.

There was a hole in the roped off section where people lined up to go through the metal detectors. It was like someone had rejiggered the line and then forgotten to close the gap.

He looked back at the lady. She was dealing with a whole family now, strollers and screaming toddlers and all.

This was his chance.

He walked coolly, casually, through the opening, got in line behind a couple making lovey-dovey eyes at each other. Tried not to freak out at what he'd just done.

And for a minute, he really thought he'd made it.

But then he heard, "Step back, sir!" and "We have a situation!" and before he could even think to get out of the line, two of the tallest and scariest TSA guys he'd ever seen had him surrounded.

"You're going to have to come with us."

Triple shit.

an iphone miracle

SAMMY'S SEAT BELT WAS BUCKLED, THE AWKWARD safety video had played, and the plane was in line for take-off. There was no turning back now.

And it was good, she told herself. Sometimes you needed to just make a freaking decision and let the cards fall. She was glad that she couldn't change things now. She was glad that she was on her way to see John.

She reached down for her purse to get a stick of gum for the flight—her ears always acted up during takeoff and landing—but when she grabbed it, her phone fell out, landing on the floor at her feet.

Somehow, the screen was lit up.

She picked up her phone. Not only was her phone on, but it had 87 percent battery. *What the hell?* she wondered. How had that even happened? Was she losing her mind?

Sammy sometimes believed that her great-grandmother was looking out for her from above, and she entertained the idea that there was life on other planets. She even sometimes thought she had a little ESP. But there was one supernatural thing that she certainly did not believe in. And that was the ability of her beat-up iPhone to magically recharge itself. Its battery life was literally the bane of her existence.

And yet, here it was, turned on and waiting for her.

She had three new texts. She tapped on the Messages icon.

One was from her roommate, Lucy, just after 5:00:

so guess who just showed up at our dorm pretty much ready to declare his love for you?

Another arrived from her ten minutes later:

i told you john was the wrong choice

And one was from, of all people, Piper, who had a phone for emergencies only. Sammy, her parents, and Gael were literally her only contacts. Sammy had never even seen Piper send a text.

hey sammy, it's piper, maybe you shouldn't get on the plane tonight, just sayin

What's more, there were three missed calls and one voice mail.

OMG.

Before she could even look at who the calls were from, the flight attendant was hovering over her. "Ma'am, I'm going to need you to put your phone on airplane mode."

"I just need to check one thing."

The flight attendant held up her hand. "Ma'am, we are already taxiing. You need to turn it on airplane mode. *Now.*"

People on either side of her were suddenly staring.

"Just let me look at this. It will take like one second, I promise."

"Ma'am, do not make me say it a third time."

"But—" Sammy didn't finish her sentence. Instead, she tapped the call log. The missed calls were from Gael.

And so was the voice mail.

"Put your phone on airplane mode, ma'am," the flight attendant said again.

"No," Sammy said defiantly. "God, just hold on a second."

The woman turned to the other attendants. "We have an unruly passenger here," she said.

Immediately, there was an announcement on the intercom. "All flight attendants please head to the back of the plane."

A rush of heels and loafers against dingy carpet.

Sammy lifted the phone to her ear.

The woman was turning as red as her polyester blazer. "Ma'am, if you do not put your phone away now, we will have no choice but to escort you off the plane."

But Sammy didn't put the phone down.

The woman's neck muscles strained against her fake silk scarf. "*Ma'am.*"

But as Sammy heard Gael's nervous voice, she didn't even care.

Let them kick her off the plane. The lady could scream at her for all she cared.

She didn't want to be on this stupid flight anyway.

tsa pda

GAEL HAD BEEN ALONE IN THE TSA HOLDING ROOM FOR forty-five minutes. It was after 8:00. Sammy's flight had definitely taken off by now, he was sitting here in hand-cuffs, and he was probably going to be charged as some sort of terrorist. His mom was very likely freaking out.

They'd confiscated his phone, so Gael couldn't even let his mom know he was okay or distract himself from the terrifying thought of what life in Guantanamo would be like.

Then, finally, the door opened. A half-bald man with tired eyes and a protruding belly walked in, a notepad in hand, looked Gael up and down, and opened his mouth to say something. But just then, voices sounded from the hall, and the man stepped back out, one hand on the door, his body hidden.

Dear god, were they recruiting someone to torture the truth out of him? Gael wondered.

"Another one?" the man asked. "Ridiculous. These enti-tled millennials. They're worse than terrorists."

He heard a muffled voice but couldn't make out the words.

"What do you mean the other room is closed for

renovations? Mike's still on break. What the hell am I supposed to do with her?"

More impossible-to-hear words, and then: "Does she seem violent?"

And after another second or two, "Fine, bring her in."

The door swung open, and Gael had to blink twice to be sure of what he was seeing. There, standing in the doorway, was Sammy Sutton.

Gael's heart threatened to burst at the seams.

She was wearing her own set of handcuffs, and she sauntered in like she owned the place.

When her eyes caught his, she gasped.

But within moments, the shocked look on her face was replaced with the most adorable smile in the world.

"Hey, stranger," she said playfully.

"Hey," Gael said.

The man looked from Sammy to Gael and back again. "You two don't know each other, do you?"

Gael shook his head quickly. Sammy did, too.

The man raised his eyebrows, but he didn't pursue it. He pulled up a chair on the other side of the table. "Take a seat," he said to Sammy. "I gotta get my partner and find another place to put you."

"Sure thing," she said. She raised her eyebrows at Gael as she sat down.

The man moved for the door. "Try not to collude or anything while I'm gone," he said. "And on a Friday, no less," he muttered under his breath as he walked out of the room.

Sammy looked behind her to make sure the door was shut. "So I didn't expect to see you here," she said. Her handcuffed hands rested on the table, just inches from his.

"Me, either," he said. He leaned forward, and so did she. They were so close it was making him crazy.

"So what's your story?" she asked, her hands magnetically moving toward his.

Gael calmed his breathing. "I was trying to get through security to convince you not to get on your flight." His hands met hers, and his thumb traced circles in her palm. His body suddenly felt hot all over. "What's yours?"

She smiled mischievously. "My phone miraculously came on just as we were about to take off. I may have been a little less than cooperative when they told me I couldn't listen to your voice mail."

Gael felt himself blush. "You shouldn't have listened to that voice mail anyway," he said. "It was terrible and awkward."

She laughed, leaned even closer. "I would expect nothing less."

"Hey," he said, without pulling back so much as a millimeter. "Not nice."

Her face was only inches from his when she spoke, so close she only had to whisper to be heard. "I'm pretty sure you never liked me because I was *nice*, Gael Brennan."

"I'm pretty sure you're right."

And then he leaned in and pressed his lips to hers.

And it was freaking fantastic.

Her lips were soft, and her mouth was warm, and it was everything he'd ever wanted, everything he hadn't even known to want just weeks before. It was exactly how it was supposed to be, he was sure of it this time . . .

Sammy pulled back. "You taste like pickles."

Gael burst out laughing. "It's a long story," he said.

"I look forward to hearing the whole thing."

He kissed her again, and it felt so wonderful, so thrilling, so *right*, that he barely even heard the opening of the door.

"Oh, Jesus Christ," the TSA man said. "I don't get paid enough to deal with this shit."

a final note from Love

AWW, DON'T YOU JUST LOVE A GOOD HAPPY ENDING?

If you're wondering if I had any role in this final push to bring these kids together, well, as a matter of fact, I did.

I may have been responsible for Sammy's phone inexplicably coming back on. And I may have handcrafted a CLOSED FOR RENOVATIONS sign on the only other interrogation room in Terminal 2.

Plus a few other tricks that need not be explained. I do have to maintain an air of mystery.

Listen, it was the least I could do after the mess I'd created.

I would never be able to make it up to Gael's parents, and maybe, in the end, that's how it was supposed to be. Maybe, as Piper reminded Gael (and me), the love they had now, though different, was still just as important. Maybe the happily ever after in store for them was a different one than I'd pictured.

I mean, if I've learned anything from this whole debacle, it's that I certainly am not always right.

Still, I had come through for Gael and Sammy.

They were on the right track, and their romance was ready to blossom.

Now, all I had to do was wait about twenty years for Gael's big movie to come out. And, believe me, I was definitely finagling premiere tickets for that one . . .

Anyway, forgive my rudeness, but I must cut my final speech a little short.

See, there's a boy in Baltimore waiting at the airport, with a teddy bear, balloons, and a heart-shaped box of chocolates in his hands. A boy who's about to have his heart broken when he realizes that Sammy won't actually be stepping off that plane.

And to be totally frank, I've got my work cut out for me again.

Because John, like Gael, is a Certified Grade-A Romantic.

Oh, dear.

Here we go again.

acknowledgments

A HUGE THANKS TO THE MANY PEOPLE (AND PLACES) who made writing this book possible.

To Annie Stone, for crazy-good insights, phone calls over the holidays, and your willingness to tackle editorial notes via text—I could not have done this without you, and I promise to (try to) take up less of your personal time in the future. And to Josh Bank, Sara Shandler, and the Alloy family—you're the brainstorming dream team I never knew I wanted. Also, a big thanks to Emilia Rhodes for taking a chance on my writing and this story. And to Danielle Rollins—our semi-regular, err, meetings at Rye turned out way more productive than either of us could have imagined!

To Anne Heltzel, for adoring my hopeless starry-eyed hero just as much as I do and believing in this book with all your romance-loving heart. And to the entire team at Abrams—you guys sure know how to make an author feel supported.

To my agent, Danielle Chiotti—you and the Upstart Crow team are rock stars. Thanks ever so much.

To the town of Chapel Hill, for taking me under its wing and giving me some of the best four years of my life. And to the crew at Cosmic Cantina: Thanks for knowing my order for four years, and sorry if I stole your hot sauce once or twice. To the "Hall of Hottness," you made Chapel Hill what it is for me.

To my mom, dad, and Kimberly—you're not only super-supportive of my writing, but you're all a bunch of movie addicts like me. Mom, thanks for exposing me to Hitchcock from a young age. Dad, thanks for taking me to all the *Star Wars*, even though the movie theater was far away. Kimberly, thanks for working through the Blockbuster horror section with me. I couldn't have written a book about a movie buff without you. And to Farley, I'm not sure if the movies we watch together get through to you, but that one time you barked your head off at the villain in *Sicario*, so I like to think they do.

Finally, to my NYC single ladies (and former single ladies)—thanks for braving the insane Brooklyn dating scene with me so I'd have lots of fodder for a romantic comedy. And to Thomas, for taking me out of said scene and never being afraid to be your own romantic self.